# DIVINE PURSUIT

## - The Divine Chronicles Book 5 -

## JoAnna Grace

ABW-WJP, LLC
P.O. Box 337
Lindale, TX 75771



2022 Cover Design by Moorbooks Design
Book design by Champagne Formats
Printed in the United States of America

Library of Congress Control Number Data
Grace, JoAnna.
Divine Pursuit / JoAnna Grace.
1. Fantasy romance—Greek mythology—Fiction. 2. Romance—Fantasy—Fiction.
3. Sagas—Romance—Fiction.
Fiction. | BISAC: FICTION / Romance / Fantasy. | FICTION / Romance / General. |
FICTION / Sagas.
PCN # 2016911679 2016
ISBN 978-1-940460-32-1
ISBN 978-1-940460-35-2 (e-book)
www.authorjoannagrace.com

# JoAnna Grace

**CONTEMPORARY ROMANCES**

*The Roles We Play*

**Riverview Romances**

*Why The River Runs*

*A River Between Us*

**PARANORMAL TITLES**

**Divine Chronicle Series:**

*Divine Awakening*

*Divine Destiny*

*Divine Judgment*

*Divine Encounter*

*Divine Pursuit*

*Divine Deception*

*Divine Justice*

**Blake Pride Series:**

*Pride Before the Fall*

*Break Her Fall*

*The Harder They Fall*

*Divided We Fall*

*Rise After the Fall*

For more information on JoAnna's books, signings, events, and more,
Sign up for the NEWSLETTER at http://eepurl.com/B_DM5!

A Note From Jo

Thank you, dear readers, for once again picking up a JoAnna
Grace novel. I hope you enjoy it. It brings me great joy to hear
from you. Please connect with me on social media:

Facebook: facebook.com/joannagraceauthor
Instagram: instagram.com/authorjoannagrace

Want updates delivered to your inbox?
Make sure you're in the know.
Sign up for my newsletter today! Visit http://eepurl.com/B_DM5

Do you want to help an author?
**Leave a review!**
Your opinion matters. Every review can help.
**Share a link to this book on social media!**
Like, follow, tag Jo, and share this book with your friends.
**Support Indie Authors**!
Did you know that an Indie Author fronts all
the cost of production?
That's right. We appreciate every person who purchases
our books because that's how we continue to produce
more. Independent authors, cover designers, editors, and
formatters work hard to bring readers quality products and
stories they can fall in love with.
Like. Share. Follow. Subscribe. Tag. Review.
It all helps the Indie community!

Share the Love.

# ACKNOWLEDGMENTS AND THANKS

First of all, thanks to each and every one of you who scream for these books! Your love for Avery and Ryse and all the Divine characters blesses me more than you know. Thanks for keeping the faith and keeping me going.

A very special thanks to Detective Laz who helped bring Brenden's skills to light in this novel. It's not every day you meet someone who can talk about dead bodies and plot murder with you. I'm excited about seeing your own book come to life and wish you the best.

Thanks to my Executive Council/Tuesday night Power Hour ladies: Mom, Cheryl, Susan, and Zana. Thank you for keeping me on task and pushing me towards the finish line. I couldn't do it without you. Love you girls!

This book is dedicated to a precious lady who blessed me with an amazing adventure this summer. Stephanie-Rose, you are a joy and a strong woman of God with a true servant's heart. Thank you for inspiring and encouraging me with your wisdom and kindness. May you be blessed ten-fold along with all my OWG Sisterhood.

# CHAPTER ONE

## HAYDEN

RYSE CASTILLE, SON OF THE GRAND DEITIES, TROY AND DYNASTY *Castille, Master of the Thracians armies and heir to the throne of North America, raised his sword. The blade shone under the watchful eyes of the gods. Zeus and all the gods of Olympia witnessed the blade fall from the sky and slice through the neck of Princess Salina Avondale, daughter of Charles and Filene Avondale, Deities of Europe.*

Hayden's hand stopped in his writing. He studied his words carefully. Zeus commanded him to record the events of the day and he wanted to do it while it was fresh on his mind. Based on the shaking in his knees and hands, it might be too fresh. It was his duty to record the events of the last few months, and as a trained historian, he enjoyed it. But this was, by far, the hardest period of Olympian history to record. Every time he closed his eyes, he could see Salina's blonde hair stained with the deep red of her blood. Bile rose in his throat when he remembered the way her head rolled across the stage and landed at the feet of her parents. Filene Avondale's screams haunted his soul. Auras of the Olympians who filled the arena flared with anger, anguish, and fear, assaulting Hayden with the battering waves of their emotions and energies.

More than any of these things, burned deeper into his brain than the color of the blood, the sound of the screams, or the waves of auras, Hayden could recall every detail about his brother, Ryse.

From the moment the Master Thracian stepped out onto the stage, the crowd quieted. Mothers pulled their children closer and ducked into the safety of their husbands' arms. Awe-filled eyes tracked his every movement and faces went slack. Ryse Castille was larger than life; he was legend made of flesh. Blessed by both Zeus and Ares, he held not only the power of Olympian royalty, but of Thracian warfare. He was part king, part killer.

Hayden inhaled deeply and let out a shaky breath. He tossed his pen aside and ran his fingers through his hair.

Not now. He couldn't relive everything just yet.

For only a moment, he wanted to sit and relax, but how could he? His big brother, the same guy he rode horses with and followed around like a puppy when they were kids, had just executed one of their childhood friends.

Zeus had handed Hayden the same position his father had held before him—not only as the Deity of North America, but as Grand Deity…over the world—and every Olympian on the planet would be under Hayden's care and protection in one month. And as if that weren't enough, finding the angel who visited him in his dreams now became imperative.

A Deity king could not reign without a Divine Grace at his side. Their union and exchange of blood bonded them into the service of the gods and their people. Their auras became as one and they merged into a powerful force.

Hayden had to find his angel. He had to locate her. But if the only time he could find her was in his dreams, he was going to have to stay unconscious for a damn month.

"I need a drink." Hayden removed his ceremonial robe and flopped down with a glass of whiskey. The library was his favorite place in the castle. Books held history, history held answers for future problems. And bloody hell, did he have a lot of problems to deal with.

He stared into the fire and thought about the biggest issues facing his people…*his* people. Not his father's. Not his brother's. His. By the gods, he prayed their biggest issue wasn't the man leading them.

The door of the library opened and in stepped his new sister-in-law, Avery. He kept his eyes on the fire, watching it dance the same way it danced in her soul. She was blessed by the sun god, Helio, and fire was one of her powers.

She sat on the edge of his chair and gave a heavy sigh. "You didn't expect that, didja?" Her Texas accent was adorable and usually thickened if she got excited or mad.

Hayden knew exactly what she meant. "No. I knew Ryse was going to turn down the North American throne, but Grand Deity. Whew." A loose strand of hair tickled his cheek and he ran his hands through it to push it back—or rip it out; he didn't care either way.

Ryse was heir to their father's throne as Deity of North America. Their family had ruled over the Olympian population in this part of the world for generations, thousands of years. Traditionally, Deity families only had one son, one heir, one rightful successor. The decision was made for them. No sibling rivalry, no bickering or fighting about who would be next, no motives to kill because some long lost fifth cousin wanted the throne. The gods anointed the family, and the only son in the family was the lucky winner.

Except for his family.

There were many rumors about how Hayden came to exist. Some Olympians believed that Hayden was a product of infidelity; some believed Ryse was. Some believed that the gods were biased and broke their own rules for the Castilles. And some believed that their family was blessed. The truth was, their lineage had anomalies. His mother was faithful to his father and his father was faithful to the gods. A second son was given to them for a purpose and now Hayden knew why.

"Kind of makes me wish I would have kept my damn mouth shut in the Heavens." He tried to joke, but his mind raced with a million thoughts all scattered about like leaves in the wind.

"You've never been able to keep your mouth shut, darlin'." Avery cupped his cheek and stared at him with green eyes that held secrets from the Heavens. Avery hadn't said too much to anyone about what truly happened to her. When Avery's soul separated from her body and went to be with the gods, she was changed forever. "Hayden, you're one of the smartest men I've ever met."

"Says the girl raised by cowboys in the backwoods of Texas. Thanks." He flinched when she tugged on his long hair.

"Shut it and listen. If anyone can lead these people, it's you."

*Please*. Hayden huffed out a breath and nearly rolled his eyes like a teenager.

"Look at me." She ran her hand across his chin. "I'm serious. Rhea and I talked about you. You're one of a kind, Hayden. You're the right blend of traditionalist and modern practice. You'll be able to help our race revive the ways of old and still usher forward a new era, a stronger one."

A few months ago, this conversation wouldn't have happened. Before her out-of-body experience, Avery knew little about the gods, their traditions, or the Olympian people. After spending time in the presence of the gods, she was suddenly an expert. "Damn, Avery, Heaven changed you."

She came sliding into his lap, surprising him with her easy affection as she kissed his cheek, showing she had come to terms with their relationship and brother and sister-in-law. "You betcha, darlin'. I think it changed you too."

It had.

It changed all of the Deities. It was one thing to read about the gods, to learn their histories in school, to feel their powers manifested within you. It was something entirely different to be in their presence, to feel their might and strength, to know how insignificant you truly were in the sight of immortals, beings that had existed when the earth was set into motion.

When he stood before the gods, before Zeus and his mother Rhea, before all the gods they worshipped, Hayden knew just what it felt like to be a bug under a microscope. The gods had just handed him the opportunity to be something more, something greater.

That didn't make it any less frightening. "You truly think I can do this?"

"I know you can. That's why I suggested you." She flashed an innocent smile that had no doubt charmed the pants right off his big brother.

"You?" That little devil. He didn't know if he should thank her or slap her. Either way, he dumped her on her rear end. "I knew having a sister was going to be a pain in my ass."

Her large, bright smile lit the room. Hayden adored Avery, and her confidence in him was astounding. How could he not smile about that? The gods had delivered Ryse a woman worthy of devotion. Surely they would do so for him as well.

"Havin' a brother ain't all it's cracked up to be either." She dusted off her butt. "Speaking of, where's yours?"

"When Ryse is upset, he usually goes to the top level of the tower. It's his place to be alone and think. I don't know if he really wants me telling you that, though. It's kind of our secret."

Avery's kind grin made his heart soften even more towards her. The love she had for his brother was her best quality, in his mind.

"I'm his mate, Hayden. We don't have secrets."

"Then you should know that the only way to get up there is through the secret door behind the tapestry. Only family knows about it."

"Thanks, love." She turned to leave the library.

"Hey, Avery? I know Salina, uh, killed you and everything…but keep in mind that we all grew up together, and Ryse doesn't like to hurt women, much less execute them."

"I know." Avery's face softened and her eyes shone with the powerful adoration she had for her mate. "That's why I'm not going to let him be alone right now. He shouldn't have to bear this burden on his own."

By the gods, Hayden prayed to find his dream woman and have her love him the way Avery loved Ryse.

If anyone could help find Hayden's love, it was Ryse. His brother had the world's best tracker and a host of other Thracians who would use their honed abilities to search every last grain of sand on earth to bring him his Divine Grace. Even as Hayden wrote about the execution, only hours ago, his mind and heart were filled with thoughts of her and the scary possibilities.

For months, she'd visited him in his dreams. An angel came to him in a white gown with long, flowing black hair and sparkling onyx eyes, flirting and smiling. Night after night, they had their encounters, learning all about one another…except for the most vital information.

Now Zeus had set a deadline.

He had a month. Only thirty short days until the gods returned to earth and celebrated his coronation. A right shoe needs a left, a lock needs a key, a king needs a queen.

It wasn't in his nature to sit still and do nothing. He rose from his chair, put his drink aside, and paced the library. What could he do? How could he help find her? How could he contribute to Ryse and Avery's fight?

*Avery.*

Yes! There was a project. Avery's blood had the power to absorb other's powers. However, there were a myriad of questions about the effects. How long did they last? Did she keep the powers permanently? Was it any Olympian power? Thracian strength?

Hayden headed down to the laboratory hidden in his wing of the castle. Science, history, the powers of the gods—these were his specialties. This was what he had to contribute. Ryse was made for fighting. Hayden was not. But the gods had given him other skills.

# CHAPTER TWO

## LYSANDRA

LYSANDRA'S VISION CAME FAST AND FURIOUS WHEN SHE TOUCHED Price Ashton's hand. The images flashed and danced in her mind, making her instantly ill.

*Long black hair, covered in blood. A child's toy lying on the floor of a hospital room, drenched in red. Female screams of agony. Begging. Pleading. Please don't do this. Pain. A woman's body mutilated, beaten and lying in the corner of a dark concrete cell. By the time Ryse arrives, it's too late.*

*A blonde this time. Scared and blind. She's crying for her family, crying for the gods' mercy. She doesn't understand why she's being taken.*

*A monster, with talons and red scaly skin, hungry for blood and power. Not of this world. Not of the underworld. A mixture of both, created by evil and birthed from dark magic.*

Lysandra excused herself and all but ran to the caravan of cars taking the Deities back to the palace. She slid into the car behind Dynasty and Hanna, holding her mouth closed.

"Are you well, child?" Dynasty asked, her brows dipping as she studied Lysa.

"Sorry, my Queen. I'm afraid the day is wearing on me." *Gods forgive me for lying.* She couldn't tell anyone what the gods revealed to her, not yet.

Kindness shined in her eyes as Dyna reached out and touched Lysa's hand. "It's understandable. Such things should not be witnessed. This is a sad day for our people."

Lysandra nodded and looked out the window as the car pulled away and Dante came running out of the arena. She laid her hand on the glass, reaching for him, but made no move to stop the car. The questioning look on his face almost broke her heart.

All she could think about were the women in her vision. If the gods gifted her with this knowledge, she had to decipher it, weed through it, and figure out what had happened and what hadn't.

Once delivered to the palace, Lysa excused herself and let Hanna know she was going for a walk to get some fresh air. Her tears slowly dripped down her face with each recollection of her vision, the execution, the whip painting Nikki's back with red stripes. Red was her least favorite color, simply because of all the blood she'd seen over the course of her visions. Decades upon decades of visions of death and destruction, mixed with beauty and majesty, weighed on her soul.

*Apollo, give me strength to carry out your will,* she prayed as she hiked.

She traveled back up the mountain to the last place she saw the demon who attacked Dante. The ground still bore the scars of the flames that held it captive. Even the trees displayed the damage. Right in the center, the earth was pitted, as if a large item had either fallen from the sky or sunk into the soil. She stepped lightly, trying not to disrupt the scene. To the right, the leaves were disturbed and covered in brown dried blood. Dante's blood.

Lysandra bent down and stretched a shaking hand towards the leaves. Maybe she could get a vision if she—

"Don't."

Lysandra sprang up and twirled around to find Dante standing in the woods, his sand-colored eyes wide and worried. Her heart lurched in surprise at seeing him, and again as she took in the sight of him, so strong and handsome. Of course he'd followed her.

"Don't touch it."

"I might get a vision—"

"You might be touching demon blood."

Lysa stepped back, her long skirts brushing against the leaves and dirt. "What would it do to me?" She approached him slowly, unsure if he was angry with her for leaving him earlier.

"I'd not risk it." Dante pulled her into the safety of his arms and she instantly felt the lack of her Olympian powers. What she did feel was the heat of Dante's chest, the strength in his arms, and the beating of his heart.

"What happened back there?" he whispered against her hair.

She wiggled deeper into his hold. "I-I had a vision when I touched the Prince."

"I know that. But why did you leave me?" He kissed her over and over again before burying his face in her hair.

"I'm not sure, to be honest. I just wanted to get far away from there. I'm sorry. Please don't be angry with me for not asking permission."

His body shook beneath her cheek. "Permission?" He chuckled. "You might not be used to this day and age yet." He tilted her chin up so he could look into her eyes. "But I don't own you. Your heart belongs to me as a gift, not as a piece of property. You don't have to stay at my heels. I was worried about you, that's all. You had a vision, and I can only imagine what you saw."

Lysa gazed deep into those sand-colored eyes that would stand out in the human world. They stood out in the Olympian world. The humans would instantly recognize them as something otherworldly. Such a shame; he had beautiful eyes.

"He's evil," she whispered.

Dante frowned. His jaw tightened. "Who?"

"Ashton. He's evil." Her voice quivered and her eyes pooled with tears.

Dante held her tighter than ever and she felt safe in his embrace. "What did you see?"

"Women, young women, beaten and dying. I saw a monster with scales and talons in a black cloak."

"Did you see Ashton?"

Lysa filtered through her vision, careful to examine every detail. "No. I didn't see him. But I recognized one of the girls, one with long black hair. I saw her when the gods gave me a vision of Yankee. She was with him, alive and happy, in love."

"With Yankee?" he scoffed. "Doubt it."

Lysa lightly tapped his chest in reprimand. "I saw it. In the vision today, she's…" Lysa closed her eyes and shuddered. "She's in danger, Dante. Whoever this woman is, she's in grave danger."

"We have to tell Ryse."

She nodded and stepped away from him. "I want to see if I can get a vision here first."

"Be mindful of where you step." Dante shadowed her around the crime scene. If he touched her, she wouldn't get a vision, so she couldn't even hold his hand while they circled and investigated.

After she'd gone over every scuffmark on the ground with no luck and no visions, she tried the trees. She touched the burned bark, she touched the singed branches, anything she could possibly get a read off of.

"Nothing. I see nothing." Visions came to her so often, it was odd not to have one at all, especially when she was concentrating so hard.

"Let's leave this place. It makes me sick." Dante rubbed at the wound on his stomach. His skin had a green tint and sweat beaded on his forehead.

"Oh, Dante, I'm so sorry. How inconsiderate of me. Yes, let's leave."

Hand in hand, they made their way back to the palace to find Ryse. After seeing him whip Nikki and behead Salina, her stomach churned at the thought of telling him any bad news.

*Apollo, grant me courage.*

Dante stopped in the middle of the forest. "Do you know where we are?"

"It all looks the same to me," Lysa confessed.

"This is the place where I first kissed you." He smiled and the world spun faster.

Lysa couldn't figure out how in the heavens she'd existed for so long without that smile. Dante was everything good in her life and more. "Perhaps, since the circumstances are better, you should kiss me again. I promise, I don't mind."

Dante's lips spread wide with his grin as he slid his hands around her waist and stepped close. She laid her hands against his chest. "I am your humble servant, my lady."

Laughter bubbled up within her and she let it flow.

Kissing was a good thing. A very good thing indeed. Kissing Dante made her whole body hum and tingle. Her breasts felt heavier, her belly clenched low. Nervous fingers traveled up Dante's neck and into his silky blond hair. Lysa tilted her head so she could better explore the divinity of his mouth. On instinct, her tongue teased at the seam of his lips and then danced with his. He put his hand on the back of her head, deepening their kiss.

Dante was her breath, her oxygen, the very meaning of her life, and she had nearly lost him. It made her appreciate him all the more.

Before she lost control of her senses, she pulled back and met his eyes.

Black eyes.

"Dante!" She jumped back.

"What? What did I do?"

Lysa covered her mouth. "Your eyes. They're black." Fear made her shiver. This had to be an effect of the demon blood that Apollo couldn't get out of him.

Dante squeezed his eyes closed. "Stay back. I don't want to take any chances with you."

"No, come on. We must go tell the others." She grabbed his hand and stopped dead in her tracks. A vision hit her hard and fast. She gasped and let the scene play out.

*An Olympian male, desperate to prove himself. A seal is broken by blood and death. Evil brings him back to life as a creature. Part demon, part Olympian. It kneels at the feet of its creator. It's hungry. A feast of Olympians at his fingertips. He's the bridge between life and death, this world and the underworld, Heaven and Hades, gods and demons. Through him, the lines have been crossed, the barriers of safety broken.*

Lysa sucked in a deep breath and fell to the ground, grasping at her throat to stop the suffocation.

"Lysandra? Lysandra, answer me." Dante shook her shoulders and when his hands touched her this time, her Olympian powers drained from her body. His eyes were back to their normal color. "What happened, Lysa?"

"I had a vision…when I touched you. I shouldn't be able to do that. How is this possible? Your eyes were black and now they're not." She panted and her eyes traveled over his face and body. "What did you do?"

Dante shook his head. "Nothing. I did nothing. I felt nothing. Well…" He blushed and couldn't meet her eyes. "I felt passion, desire. But nothing negative." He helped her to her feet. "What about you? Did you notice anything, except for my eyes?"

"No. I'm frightened, for you. Please, we have to go tell the Deities. Perhaps you should see a Paean?"

"If Apollo couldn't cleanse the demon blood from me, I doubt an Olympian healer can." Dante stared at the ground and shoved his hands in his pockets. "Let's go."

They didn't speak as they hiked back down the mountain and to the palace. The first thing they did was seek out a well-known Paean and scientist named Christophe. He drew Dante's blood and checked him over from the top of his head to the bottom of his feet. Christophe's gift allowed him to recognize the Olympian magic in blood and analyze the various powers gifted from the gods.

"I'll take a look at it more closely as soon as I can. Prince Hayden has me working on something right now, but…" He snapped his fingers as his eyes lit with an idea. "Your blood might actually help me with it. Do you mind if I use a few drops for another experiment?"

"I suppose not." Dante kicked his head to one side.

"You are a guardian of our Lady, are you not?" Christophe was already sucking blood out of the vial with a dropper and placing it in a petri dish.

Dante lifted his chin and Lysa's heart pinged with pride. "I am."

"Then I suppose you will be blood bound to her soon enough. Better safe than sorry," he mumbled under his breath. He was already leaning over his microscope and squinting into the lenses. "I'll let you know what I find."

Without any more than that for dismissal, Lysa and Dante turned towards the exit. Again, Lysa was hit with a vision. Nothing violent this time, but still disturbing. In a second, she knew all about how Christophe had discovered the miracle in Avery's blood, how Princess Salina had brainwashed him, how he nearly lost his family because of it. She also saw his intelligence and his loyalty to the Deities and gods. Christophe was a man who could be trusted.

"Another vision?" Dante asked as he guided her down the hall.

"Yes. It's rather irritating; when I need a vision, they cease. When I don't need them, they flow like springs."

"Do I want to know what this one was about? I did just give this man my blood." Dante rubbed the crease of his elbow and pursed his lips. A silly, almost teasing twinkle lit his eyes when she suppressed a smile.

Lysa took his hand, happy to feel the relief from her magic for a moment. "He is a devoted follower of the gods. You needn't worry, my brave warrior." With a heavy sigh, she leaned her head on his shoulder. "There are much worse individuals than Christophe out there. And I'm afraid it's time to tell Master Ryse about my other visions."

# CHAPTER THREE

## ASHTON

ASHTON PICKED UP HIS CELL PHONE AS HIS FAMILY TRAVELED TO the airport to head back to England. His mother, Filene, sniffled and wiped her nose, still crying over her daughter's murder. She faced one window; his father, Charles, faced the other with not a tear in his eyes. One fist was clenched tight against his lap, the other against his mouth as he leaned on the car door.

The text was from one of his spies in the field. "Asset one is under surveillance, asset two and three are located. Retrieval set. Assistance needed. Chicago."

Bloody hell, they'd found them. Satisfaction coursed through his veins. He would have a teleporter again. His trackers and spies had been watching the compound of Evander Castille for years; waiting, observing. Up until recently, the compound—which housed a clinic for muddy-blooded Olympians—had only hosted a few Thracians and people coming to the clinic. In the last couple months, the number of Thracian guards had increased and a maid reported two women—twins—taking up residence in the mansion. One was working in the clinic, the other was Evander's toy.

Ashton didn't care about the healer. Paeans were fairly easy to find. The other one, however, intrigued him. His spies were everywhere, including inside Evander's home. A maid, whose son was taken as leverage, had reported seeing the one girl disappear out of thin air, taking Evander with her. Later, they reappeared with wet hair and sand on their clothing, laughing about palm trees and margaritas.

He sent back a text to his man in Chicago. "Will arrive shortly. Prepare." Instead of heading straight overseas, he would have to make a pit stop.

"I need to go visit some of Salina's friends. They should hear the truth from me. I'll be home as soon as I can be."

"Salina had friends?" Charles said on top of his mother's, "They will be devastated."

Filene glared at her husband. "Of course Salina had friends, or followers, I should say. People all over the globe loved our daughter. It's fitting for her brother to console them." She gave Ashton a tight, tear-filled smile. "That's kind of you, son. Perhaps you can rally support to our family."

"For what?" Charles snapped. "To our cause? What cause? Our daughter defied the gods, cursed and mocked them, murdered my best friend, and paid the price for her sins. The only cause people should be rallying to is the cause of the gods. Our family should be begging their mercy."

"Mercy?" Filene's voice was a hoarse screech. She slapped her fist on the leather seat. "Where was the gods' mercy today, Charles? Where? Our daughter is dead. Our little girl is gone, and Ryse Castille killed her. You know how she loved him. From the time she was a child, she followed him around, pining for him all her life, and he betrayed her." Filene covered her face with a handkerchief and cried. "They betrayed us all."

Charles sighed and turned back to the passing cityscape. "You're in shock. You don't know what you're saying."

Ashton sat quietly during the argument. The seeds of hate for the Castilles were planted nice and deep within his mother. With a little cultivation, they would grow fast and mighty.

"Okay then," he said, breaking the awkward silence. "I'll meet you both at home."

Not another word was said until his parents boarded a private jet to New York, then England, and he boarded a private plane to Chicago. This flight was off the books.

"Xavier." Ashton snapped his fingers. The seasoned warrior came to the back of the plane and sat in one of the leather seats, facing his prince. "Did you speak to your son before you left?"

Thin lips pursed. His sand-colored eyes narrowed. "Briefly. Dante was positioned so far up Ryse's arse, I didn't get much of a chance, and then he had that Oracle at his side."

Ashton sat with his legs crossed at the knees. He rolled up his sleeves and loosened the collar of his shirt. "And what do you think about that?"

"A reject Thracian would attract a reject Oracle." He shrugged it off and leaned back to mirror Ashton's casual position. "If she were of importance, she'd be in Delphi with the other smoke-headed nutcases."

"What about the fact that Apollo himself healed your son?"

Xavier's bushy salt-and-pepper-colored brows dipped low. "Have you suddenly taken a liking to the boy? If you think he has value, I'll permit him—"

"No, no." Ashton waved off the idea. "I don't need him. Like you said, he's tied up with the Castilles now. What I'm trying to determine is your…" He searched for the right word before he met Xavier's eyes again. "…sentimentality towards him."

"You are my master."

Ashton leaned over and put his elbows on his knees. "They

killed my sister, Xavier. Do you understand what position they've put me in?"

"Yes," the older man growled.

"You fancied Salina, didn't you? I know she visited you more than once…*privately.*"

The truth was written all over Xavier's face. His tense jaw nearly dropped to the floor. Ashton was no fool and he kept abreast of all his sister's activities, especially when they involved Xavier. The General didn't necessarily love Salina, but he enjoyed her company and her unique brand of pleasures. As much as she spread her legs for anyone, Salina had a preference for Xavier too.

"Don't worry, old man." Ashton smirked. "She told me you were her choice if Father ever forced her to marry."

A single brow raised on Xavier's forehead. "And my current wife?"

"She doesn't have to know," said Ashton. "I would've made it happen, but since it's not an option now, your wife doesn't need to know anything. I know her interests do not align with ours, but divorce is ugly, even in our world, and it's not like you're mated like Deities."

Xavier took a deep breath and turned to face the window. "I have more evolved appetites now. Elaine gave me many daughters and finally one son who is less than acceptable. She was good for a time, but her season is over."

"I'm glad we are on the same page, Xavier. I can promise you, when I rule all of the Olympians on this planet, you will be my General, not Gaston. He is loyal to my father and he will remain with him. I need my own men. I need you. You have my word."

Xavier's eyes lit with ambition. "I will serve by your side, sire. Anything you ask, I will do."

*Gotcha.* Xavier was ripe for the picking. His desire for power was his greatest strength and his greatest weakness.

"And your other children?" Ashton tilted his head to the side as Xavier squirmed in his seat.

"Daughters. What does a soldier need with daughters?" He swallowed hard, the only sign that he might be worried about his children.

Ashton drummed his fingers on his knee, making sure his body language conveyed exactly what he wanted it to. "I think we need to protect them." Xavier's shoulders relaxed fractionally and Ashton continued, "If you are my General, your daughters will be targets. You love them, old man. Any red-blooded male should be proud of his children. It might be easy to write off Dante, but your daughters love their father."

Xavier had a constipated expression on his face, pinched and pained. "They would make fine wives to our soldiers. They are… well-raised women." The fact that he wanted to hide his pride for his daughters only made them more valuable in the grand scheme of things.

Ashton chuckled. "Oh, come on. It's me." He gently slapped a hand against Xavier's knee. "I know you. Loving your heirs is not a crime or a weakness. Say the word and I'll have bodyguards on them right now. If they are special to you, they are special to me."

It took a moment of clear indecision, but finally, Xavier gave him a thin smile. "It would set my mind at ease to know they are watched over, sire."

"Done." Ashton smiled brightly and leaned back in his chair, offering Xavier a flask of whiskey. "Now, let's talk about who awaits us in Chicago."

The two men exchanged knowing grins. Yes, Xavier was his. The Castilles had slighted him more than once by denying him Elite status and then assigning him to be the guardian of a prince and not the General of Europe. Now they'd taken away his favorite toy by murdering Salina. The love of his daughters was a weakness, for sure. Ashton wanted Xavier unattached and unencumbered by affections and loyalties aside from those he had for his prince. One way or another, he would have to prove himself.

While they were on a plane, one of Ashton's men had already been tailing the oldest two of Xavier's daughters for months, wiggling himself into their lives. At any moment, the man knew he could be called up to snatch the girls and use them as leverage. Ashton didn't care about Elaine. The wife could die as far as he was concerned. The oldest girls, however, were pawns in his game, even if no one knew it yet.

# CHAPTER FOUR

## NIKKI

THE SUN ROSE WARM AND BRIGHT ON NIKKI'S FACE. FOR A MOMENT, she thought about how beautiful it was, how good the rays felt on her skin. She reached up to push the hair away from her cheeks.

Then the pain set in. She gasped and whimpered.

Every nerve and muscle burned like fire from the base of her neck to the bottom of her spine. The lashes had left a macabre pattern of stripes on her skin. The Paeans had healed her as best they could, but her scars remained. The muscles and skin were still healing, but only time would help.

"What do you need? Are you hurting?" a sleepy voice whispered beside her.

Nikki carefully turned her head to see Brenden on her bed beside her. "What are you still doing here? Soldiers are not—"

"Ryse commanded I take care of you." He brushed the hair from her face and rolled up on his side to push her mass of hair away from the bandages across her back. Blue eyes scanned her body.

"I'm surprised."

Bren placed a kiss on her bare shoulder. "He did what he had to do. We both know he didn't like it or even agree with it." His jaw tensed and his eyes held a quiet anger that made her worry about where he placed his blame.

"The gods have a purpose for everything, Bren. They will not waste my pain. If you want to be angry with someone, be angry with Salina or the Rogues. Be angry with those who deserve it."

He shook his head. "How can you be so forgiving? Ryse is my master, but I still wish I could cut off his hand for whipping you."

Nikki ran her fingers up his arm and took his hand, intertwining their fingers. "At this moment, I'm not his biggest fan." She tried to smile, but her eyes misted over. "But we have a duty to Avery. I don't know what that looks like anymore." Her voice cracked. "You said you would help me find myself again."

"I will." He kissed her forehead. "I promise I will, Nikki."

There was no way to move without hurting, but Nikki pushed herself up and brought the sheet to cover her breasts. She cringed with each tiny movement; her skin stretched and the wounds argued in pain.

"Stop." Brenden lifted a hand to stop her. "What are you doing? Lie back down."

"I need you to find a Paean. I'm going to create a shirt with cooling compresses in the back and we are going out there." Nikki pointed at the door. "I have to know if I still belong, Brenden, and I can't do that from this room."

"You're not healed yet."

"Hence the need for a Paean. Please."

Brenden took a heavy breath and scrubbed his hands through his blond hair. "Okay. Yes, ma'am. Breakfast?"

"Please."

With a nod of his head, Brenden rose and made for the door. He stopped, half outside. "Nikki."

She turned her head, which pulled on her scars at the top of her spine.

"You're still the most beautiful woman in the world." He closed the door and heat crept up her face.

Once she was alone, Nikki used very little of her powers to conjure and create a black button-up shirt with built-in cooling packs all along the backside. She would look like a humpback for a while, but at least she could be with Avery.

Salina might have robbed her of her title of Shadow Lady, but she could not rob her of her devotion to her mistress. Nikki stood in the bathroom, looking at herself in the mirror.

"You don't have to have a title to fulfill your duty. You don't have to have a title to fulfill your duty."

She repeated the mantra over and over again until she began to believe it.

The Paeans came in and gave her some much needed respite from the pain. The skin was now closed over the lashes, knitted back together thanks to the magic of their healing hands. Once she overcame this physical pain, she could focus on the mental. For now, she just wanted to show everyone that she could still be by Avery's side.

All her life, all she had ever wanted to do was serve a Deity. Since the time she was a little girl, her mother and father had been against it, wanting nothing more than to secret away her talent and use it for their own gain. Nikki wanted more. She groomed herself to be the perfect Shadow Lady and everything the name implied. Nikki went to classes for every manner of etiquette and the duties of Shadow Ladies.

*We are the shadow of the Queen.*
*We are her servant and caretaker.*
*We always follow and sometimes guide.*
*We kneel to her, yet stand firmly behind her.*

*We are the voice of reason or the silence in which she thinks.*
*We are her maid, her assistant, her confidant, her friend.*
*We are a shield between our mistress and those who wish her harm.*
*We are servants of the gods, wholly devoted to their will.*
*We are the shadows of the Queen.*

Nikki took those vows on her graduation day in this very Haven. She was the top of her class and already working as a maid in the palace. Scrubbing toilets, washing floors, shining the silver, sweeping the many porches and decks, it didn't matter—Nikki was simply blessed to be there and she never complained. When news of Avery's arrival hit, everyone knew Nikki would be the first choice. Queen Dynasty handpicked her for her sunny disposition.

She didn't feel so sunny today.

Nikki shrugged on her shirt and buttoned it up. The cooling packs stuck out, so she kept her hair down for a change. If she pulled it back into her usual ponytail, the lumps would be obvious. Movement down the hall signaled it was time to get to work. She took a deep breath before opening the door to her room.

*I can do this. I can do this.*

The first step outside her door ran her smack into Master Ryse. "Nikki?"

"My apologies, Master." She bowed her head low.

"What are you doing up? How—you should be resting, healing."

The concern in his voice helped ease her pain, but it was still hard to look at his face, the face of the man who only yesterday had brought her so much agony. "I cannot serve the gods from my bed, sire."

"No, but you need time—"

"With all due respect, my lord, I need to keep myself busy. Unless that is a command?"

She glanced up and up into his hard face, yet his eyes were wide and his brows rose high on his forehead. "Uh, no, I suppose not. Avery is in our room."

"Thank you, Master." Nikki bowed and turned away from him. "Nikki?"

She closed her eyes and slowly turned around. "Yes, Master."

"My father always told me that a good king recognizes when he is wrong." His nostrils flared and his eyes stared straight at her. "I have wronged you, even in the service of the gods. Even knowing you had no voluntary part in my father's death, I was angry with you, but I never wanted to punish you. I—I ask for your forgiveness."

Her chin quivered as she knelt down at Ryse's feet. "I shall forever be in your service. You have done nothing against me, though I greatly wounded you—"

"Nikki, you didn't—"

"I did. I hurt you and your entire family. The pain I have suffered is not enough, though I thank the gods for sparing me when they did. From now, until the end of my days, I will serve you, Master, and my mistress. I…" She choked up at her next admission. "I am no longer a Shadow Lady by title and rank, but I still wish to stay by Avery's side. It's all I've ever known, all I've ever wanted, and I love her so dearly."

"I know you do. She would burn every hair on my head if I said no." He held out his hand to help her to her feet. A tight smile spread over his face. "Your honor will be rewarded, in this life or the next."

"May the gods bless you, Master."

"And you." Ryse lifted his chin and looked down at her with kindness in his brown eyes. "Now, if you will please go get my lovely wife out of bed, I expect her and a few others to be in the conference room in an hour."

Nikki nodded quickly, happy for the order, happy to serve. "Yes, sire."

Avery gave her the same concern. "Why are you out of bed? Get your rear end back in there and rest."

"My master has given me orders."

"I don't care what he did. You're not in any shape to be up and working." Avery examined her face, her hands, the cooling packs in her shirt. "Your hair is pretty down like that. Dang it, Nikki. You're hurtin' my heart. You never wear your hair down and I know darn well it's to hide that shirt."

"Avery, please," she begged in a shaking whisper.

Avery nodded her head, her lips pinched together, and her aura flashed with affection and concern and fear.

The two women prepared and made their way down the hall to the conference room of the palace. They were met by the Queen, Dynasty, and her Shadow Lady, Hanna. As the four of them walked past the east wing entrance, Lysandra joined them.

"You too?" Avery asked the Oracle.

"Yes, Mistress. It seems we have all been summoned." Lysandra smiled at her, her eyes shining with kindness. "Good morning, Nikki. I'm so very happy to see you up and moving today."

"As am I," chimed in Dynasty.

"Me, too," Hanna said at the same time.

"Thank you, ladies." Their forgiveness and kindness only made Nikki bow her head lower. People should not forgive her so easily. Her hands delivered the poison that killed a king, a Grand Deity, a father and husband.

The sight of Troy dying would forever be burned into her brain right along with the terror of her trial before the gods and the agony of Ryse's lashes. Her back ached just thinking about it.

Before she opened the door, Avery took a deep breath and sent them a strained smile that said, "Here we go." Avery and Dynasty entered the room first, Lysandra next, and Nikki waited until Hanna had entered before she snuck in behind the group. What if the Elites didn't want her there? Avery, yes, but not her? Not the traitor. Not the murderer. Not the outcast. Nikki kept her head down. Gods, but she was frightened to be in the same room with them all.

"Stop it," Avery whispered to her. "I feel your aura." She reached back and took Nikki's hand.

Nikki nodded but kept her head low and her mouth silenced.

"Gentlemen," Ryse said, commanding all the attention in the room, thankfully. "I have asked these ladies to join our council this morning. We have a few things to discuss and I believe all of them should be included." He opened his hand to the empty chairs about the room.

Relief settled in as Avery took her seat and pulled out the one next to her for Nikki. Ryse started talking, but Nikki took this moment to look around the room. It was full of the Elites and other Thracian soldiers. Tall, brooding men with scowls on their faces and death on their minds.

Except one.

Brenden met her eyes and winked, then turned to Ryse.

As much as she dreaded his affections now, her heart still fluttered when his blue eyes locked on hers. Loving her would be his biggest mistake, and yet, he was willing.

"We face a new threat." Ryse's hands fisted. "All this time, we've been so focused on rogue Olympians, that we have missed the real enemy." He took a deep breath. "And he is at our door."

The men all sat a little straighter, their eyes focused more. Even Nikki found herself more alert at his warning.

"Demons have found a way out of the underworld…"

Nikki closed her eyes and took a deep breath. After her time in the Heavens, coming face to face with Hades himself, the thought of anything spawned from his likeness made her stomach drop. After her trial, the god of the underworld had looked deep inside her, down to the root of her soul, and saw everything that existed in her mind and heart. He saw her memories, her fears, every lie she'd told—intentional or otherwise—every sin she'd committed, every moment of doubt and desperation, every moment of joy and happiness. In a millisecond, he knew everything about her…and she about him.

Hades' soul was filled with the void of all light and happiness. For all the goodness and love the gods possessed, Hades possessed a richer, darker evil. He triumphed in nightmares and delighted in torture. His spawn would turn this earth upside down and inside out, leaving nothing but destruction and blood.

Dynasty glanced over at her, catching her attention. Nikki met the Queen's incredible lavender eyes. They flashed a brilliant white, quick as lightning, then turned purple again.

She knew.

"Hades has always hated us." Dynasty sighed. Nikki's knowledge was now hers. "Since our beginning, Hades has been jealous. He thought that by creating demons as his spawn, they would give him the same devotion that Olympians give to Zeus. But because he is cruel and hateful, they turned against him. Now he wants nothing more than for Olympians to be destroyed out of jealousy."

Nikki listened to the back and forth, a heavy weight gathering in her chest. Zeus had given Prince Hayden a little less than one month to find his Divine Grace. That task had taken Ryse decades. Hayden had one month until his coronation, one month to do what took others years.

The Oracle, Lysandra, had also been given news of Hayden's Divine Grace. Whatever she had to say made her fidget and twitch. Dante touched her knee to calm her, but she still shook as she spoke.

"If you don't find her in the next month, she'll be dead. Ashton will find her and eventually kill her."

While the outraged men in the room grumbled and growled, Nikki kept her eyes on Hayden. His skin paled and his eyes widened. His mouth dropped open and his chest moved in short spurts, like he was having trouble breathing. The look of desperation on his face broke her heart.

Dynasty stood up so quickly, her chair nearly fell over. Hanna grabbed it before it hit the floor. The Queen slammed her fist on the table. "Over my dead body." Her voice came out feral and full of anger. Nikki's body shivered and shrank back in her seat as Dynasty took on a white glow, the power of the gods called up by her wrath.

Everyone in the room was as shocked as Nikki was at Dynasty's outburst. Brenden's mouth hung open, one side of Yankee's mouth pulled back into a satisfied smirk, and even Cutter's eyes widened—and he never showed any such emotions.

"I've had enough of those cursed Avondales bringing pain to my family. First my husband, now my sons and their wives. No." Her fists stayed balled up and her spine straightened. Dynasty squared her shoulders, looking as regal and majestic as Nikki had ever seen her. "No more. I will not sit on the sidelines one more minute. I will fight with my last breath to bring this girl home."

Not many people knew that Dynasty and her departed husband, Troy, often dueled together, sword to sword. It had been many decades since the Queen picked up a blade, but she was adept in using one.

"So shall I," Hanna said, ever the dutiful Shadow Lady, standing behind her mistress, even if it risked her own life.

Lysandra stood next to pledge her allegiance. "I'm not much of a fighter, but I believe my skills of precognition could be useful in a battle situation. I will do anything you ask of me."

Nikki had to hand it to her; the Oracle didn't seem afraid at all. Meanwhile, Nikki was about to shake out of her clothes. She knew what was coming, and she knew what she must do.

On cue, Avery stood with the rest of the women. "Y'all know I'm not afraid to rush into the middle of trouble. At least this time, I'm a bit more prepared." Fire ignited from her hand with control and skills.

*When did she learn to do that?*

It seemed she needed to have a serious talk with Avery about what happened before her trial. Suddenly, she was manifesting fire and talking about kicking ass. She was the last woman sitting and she met Hayden's eyes. One single brow lifted slightly on his forehead. A challenge?

"I want to fight." Nikki stood up on impulse. The words escaped her before she had the chance to realize how frightened she was. All the men stared at her. She swallowed the knot in her throat and heat climbed up her neck into her face. Her eyes drifted to the floor. "But I—I will have to be taught."

Brenden was next to her in a blink. "You don't have to do this. You have nothing to prove here."

It was bad enough that everyone was questioning her mental state, now Brenden questioned her loyalty. No matter how much she wanted to, she would not give in and cry. She grit her teeth and turned her anger on him. "I have *everything* to prove. This has nothing to do with you. I serve Avery and if my mistress steps up to fight, I will be at her side. Just as you will be." Nikki had just as much right to protect Avery as he did, and he didn't need to forget it. Brenden's head dipped and he cursed under his breath.

Avery was right. It was time for the Olympians to remember that the gods didn't create them to sit by idly while Thracians, like Brenden, gave their lives to save them. The gods had given all their children gifts and powers, not just the Thracians. Nikki's gift of conjuring could be of great value. Anything they needed in the field, she could create it. Bandages, bullets, even cars.

Yes, she would avenge her own name and title. She would prove to everyone that no matter what Salina implanted in her head, Nikki was a true Shadow Lady, and Shadow Ladies did whatever was necessary to serve their mistresses.

# CHAPTER FIVE

## AVERY

Some of the most powerful people in the planet sat in a conference room that morning, and yet, some of the most powerful beings in the universe were their adversaries. Avery held the mighty power of flames within her, but she was no match for demons. She'd been schooled by Helios, the god of fire, during her visit to the Heavens, but she was no match for Hades. Even as she stood with others in unity, a ball of fire dancing in her palm, fear crept into her mind.

Hayden discovered that her blood could absorb powers. But what did that really mean? How? Did they last? Did they fade after a certain amount of time? Was her sponge-like blood the key to their victory?

Hell if she knew.

Their meeting broke up and Hayden approached as if he'd read her mind. "Come, sister dearest."

"Why? So you can dump me on the floor again?"

His eyes twinkled, a small spark of hope among all the bad news. "Don't tempt me, hillbilly. We're going to do some testing. Nikki, would you like to be my lovely assistant?"

"Yes, Prince. Whatever you ask of me."

"For what?" Brenden butted in to the conversation, his hand going protectively to the small of Nikki's spine.

"I have to see what's going on with Avery's blood and powers. It's not enough to play in the lab. We have to see what happens to her. I figured Nikki's blood would be the safest."

"Why not mine or Dante's? Why not Ryse? He's her mate."

Avery held up a hand to stop Brenden's questioning. "First off, I've been to the afterlife and back, and still don't like the term 'mate.' Second, Nikki's power makes sense. It's not harmful. What's the worst that can happen? I gain her powers and manifest a hundred chocolate cakes?"

"I wouldn't complain," Nikki mumbled, a sign of her old sense of humor coming out. Even Bren's lips pulled back into a tiny smile.

"Exactly," Hayden said. "Ryse's blood is too powerful, your gift is uncontrollable and wild, especially for someone who has never experienced it firsthand, and Dante's gift would erase all her powers. I figured starting with Nikki would be safest."

Avery rubbed her hands together. "Let's do this. You want us to do the magic cup thingy that Ryse and I did?"

Hayden scrunched up his face. "I'm afraid this is going to be much more…clinical."

*Dang it.*

Twenty minutes later, Avery lay on one hospital bed and Nikki on her stomach beside her, tubes running between them and machines.

To take her mind off of it, Avery did exactly what she did when Dynasty was unlocking her aura—she recited cooking directions.

"To make the perfect Italian cream cake, you need one cup of buttermilk, one teaspoon of baking soda, one-half cup of butter…"

"Please tell me someone is writing this down," Ryse called over his shoulder as he stood next to her bed and held her hand. He smiled down at her and, for a moment, she forgot what came next in her recipe. *Thank you, gods, for that smile and the man who blesses me with it.*

All the Elites came down to the lab to watch the transfusion. If she could absorb others' powers and keep them, Avery would be a big gumbo of all their gifts.

And if she had some weird reaction and manifested a thong or something, they would have ammunition to tease her with for all time. It was a win either way for them.

She kept reciting the steps of baking while the transfusion took place. Nikki didn't make a sound next to her until Avery was done with her recipe and the healers bandaged them up.

Nikki finally released a heavy breath. "After this, you must make me that blasted cake."

Brenden was at her side, helping her sit up as Ryse helped Avery.

"Anything?" One of his dark brows rose.

Avery shrugged. She felt normal at the moment, a bit queasy from the process, but nothing too out of the ordinary. "How do I do this? How do we test it?"

All eyes went to Nikki. Her eyes darted around and landed on the floor. "Um, okay, when I want to manifest something, I concentrate on the cellular makeup, the textures, the parts. When I visualize it, the object appears. Think of something."

"Well, right now, my mind is on cake. So let's start there." Avery relaxed her shoulders and held out her hands in front of her as if she were ready to hold a cake. She closed her eyes and thought about the texture, about the way it smelled when she first took it out of the oven.

Her hands twitched. A white glow clouded her vision.

She considered the frosting and the way it spread on the cake.

Her hands tingled. She concentrated on each ingredient and how they came together to create pure perfection.

Scents of cream and sugar filled the room as it formed in her palms. Avery opened her eyes and laughed out loud as the cake formed to completion, then crumbled in her hands. "I guess I should also conjure a tray next time."

Everyone laughed—until the cake caught on fire.

"Shit!" Avery dropped it and Nikki conjured a fire extinguisher to put out the flames. She looked to Hayden. "What does that mean? That can't be good."

He grimaced. "Humph. Perhaps it's your body adjusting?"

"Adjustin'?" Avery's voice pitched high. "I just burned a perfectly good cake."

Go figure; Yankee bent down, ran his finger through the burned icing, and stuck it in his mouth. "Not bad. A little charred, but not bad."

"Don't eat that, moron," Brenden said.

"I want to try again." Avery held out her hands and imagined a book. Everyone else in the room stepped back just in case. The book formed in her palms. She sat still, waiting for the book to go up in flames. Nikki held the extinguisher at the ready.

Nothing happened. "This is a good sign, right?"

No one moved.

"What?" Avery noticed them all staring. "*What?*"

Yankee chuckled, but wide-eyed Nikki held up a finger pointed at her head. Avery flinched. "My hair is on fire, isn't it?"

Nikki nodded.

"Dang it!" She shook her head and the flames went out, leaving her deep red hair unharmed. "One more time." She put the book on the floor, closed her eyes, and held out her hands to try again. This time, she thought about something more intricate, more challenging; something that would take her whole concentration. She thought about a clock.

When she was a child, she could remember her father taking apart a tabletop clock. It was a beautiful piece of craftsmanship with all its moving parts and shining cogs. The clock had stopped working and he'd had to fix it. Her father took his time, disassembling and laying out each piece in the order he removed it.

"You know, Avery," he had said, "the world is a bit like this clock. All the pieces are made to work in sync with each other. That's the way we were created, to all work together. All it takes…" He pulled a piece of splintered wood, likely from one of his carpentry projects, and held it up with a pair of tweezers. "…is one splinter in society to make things quit working."

Her father then carefully assembled the clock and got it back to working.

His lesson stuck with her and so did the pieces of that clock.

Avery opened her eyes and in her hands was an exact replica of her father's clock. Breath expelled from her lungs and she nearly cried, right there in front of everybody.

"Anything on fire?" Her voice shook.

"Not yet," Brenden answered.

Here was a memento in her hands that was exactly like the one belonging to her father. It even had the dent on the top of the wood from where she'd dropped it as a child. Everything she loved and cherished about her parents had been burned in the fire that started the night she learned the truth about who and what she was. Yet she held an exact replica of her father's clock.

"Such a wonderful gift you've got, Nikki." Avery sent her a watery smile.

"Yes, Mistress."

Hayden came over and picked up the book, examined it, picked up the clock, examined it. Each page was turned, the clock set and working. He pricked Avery's finger to see how her blood was reacting to the new recipe.

"Okay, okay, enough." Avery slapped him on the shoulder.

"I've been your lab rat enough for today, thanks." She rose from the examining table and took a deep breath.

Hayden was already preparing his experiments and taking notes. "Don't push yourself too hard. We don't know how your body will react over time. You should stay close in the palace."

"What do I do if something goes wrong?" Avery turned to Ryse, who had his arms crossed over his chest, one hand rubbing his chin. He shrugged a shoulder.

"Thus far," Hayden said, "we have no reason to believe that the mixture of magics has a negative effect. Your blood seems to mix fine and even changes your DNA structure to reflect each new gift. As of now, none of the tests we've run have been worrisome. That's not to say you might not get sick or have a reaction, so like I said, stay close and don't exert yourself."

"Got it. Go take a nap." She yawned, right on time, as if she hadn't just woken up a few hours ago.

"The transfusion probably made you tired. You should rest." Ryse took her hand and they headed down the hall and up the stairs to the ground level of the palace.

"I feel fine, really. Can we go over some basics? We are supposed to be learnin' how to fight, ya know."

Ryse nodded. "Yankee, Brenden, Dante, Cutter, let's take the ladies to the shooting range. The least we can do today is get them familiar with some simple firearms, maybe knives, Cutter. Teach them how to defend themselves."

Nikki was kind enough to conjure simple black pants and shirts to change into. Even Dynasty and Hanna, who hadn't worn anything but long dresses since the first time she'd arrived, changed into the cotton pants.

"I have to say," Dynasty pulled at the legs of her pants, "my husband would never believe this. Except for when we rode horses, I don't believe I've ever worn pants."

"Ever?" Lysandra asked. "Even I've worn them a time or two

since I've been here." She worked to pull her long black hair into a ponytail. Nikki ended up helping her by braiding it and then wrapping it in a bun on the back of her head. Her fingers made such quick work of it that Lysa was surprised when she touched the bun. "Oh my, thank you very much."

"Not once in many years." Dynasty, too, tried to pull her knee-length blonde hair back. "Nikki, will you do me the honor?"

Nikki's olive green eyes darted from Hanna to Avery. It was something Hanna should've done for her mistress, yet the Queen asked *her*. "Y-yes, my lady."

Dynasty faced Avery as Nikki stepped behind her to twist one long, thick braid. She winked.

Avery suppressed a smile. Everyone was being most gracious to Nikki and that made all the difference in the world.

When Nikki was done, the Queen brought the long, intricate braid over her shoulder to inspect it. "Perfect, wouldn't you say, Hanna?"

"Yes, perfect." Hanna tipped her head to Nikki.

Nothing that came from Hanna's lips could be taken lightly, or so Ryse had explained. Hanna had the gift to voice action and truth. Her gift had a price attached with every usage. If Hanna gave a command as simple as wash the dishes, you would go straight to the kitchen. She wouldn't have feeling in her fingertips for a week afterward, but her power would prevail.

For her to say something was perfect and have no recourse meant Nikki had done a fine job indeed.

Dynasty, Hanna, Lysa, Avery, and Nikki followed the Thracians down to the indoor gun range. Ryse and Avery stepped into one stall, Dynasty and Yankee into another. Cutter and Lysa went next door with Brenden and Nikki to work on knife throwing.

"I know how to shoot a gun, Ryse. I'm from Texas. My daddy taught me and then Frank drilled me like one of his police trainees." Avery loaded the pistol he'd selected for her with ease. "I'm sure you remember the stash I had in my house."

"I do." He took the gun and completely disassembled it. "I want you to conjure one just like this one."

"Hayden said—"

"I know what he said, but he doesn't know you like I do. You have to emotionally engage with your powers before they will work. You're better, different but better, after your training with Helios."

"Ryse." Avery touched his cheek and looked up into his brown eyes, so full of concern. "I don't know if I'll ever be able to explain to you what happened in the Heavens, with Rhea and Helios, and even Athena, but I don't want you to worry. They've prepared me."

He took her hand and kissed her palm, breathing in the scent of her wrist. "I never want to lose you again. Now I fear my brother will lose his woman. Hammon and Philippe are working on narrowing down our search, but what if we don't—"

"Don't say it." Avery pulled him close. "We won't fail Hayden. We won't fail her, wherever she is." She rose on her tip-toes and kissed him, running her hands up his strong shoulders and into his long black hair.

That was all it took to set her insides on fire. Ryse's lips were the most decadent of pleasures. She loved the way he was as enraptured as she was. He pulled her closer and gripped her bottom, his other hand on the back of her neck.

"I don't hear any gunfire from over there," his mother said from behind the wall. She cleared her throat and Ryse and Avery both turned to see her leaning around the wall, smirking. Yankee was right behind her.

"Get a room." Yankee rolled his eyes.

"Focus, you two." Dynasty's scolding was eased by her smirking giggle. They went back to their stall.

Ryse's eyes sparkled with love when he grinned at her. "I'll never get enough of you," he whispered and kissed her again. "But my mother is right; we should focus."

An hour later, they switched. Avery and Dynasty, who was quite proficient with a gun, went to Cutter and Dante for knife training. And Nikki and Lysa came to Ryse and Yankee for shooting.

"I'm keeping my homemade guns." Avery smirked as she showed Nikki, who walked up.

Nikki squared her shoulders and looked Ryse directly in the eyes. It took everything she had not to squirm. No one looked Ryse in the eyes. She swallowed hard.

"I don't need to learn guns, Master."

"Yes, I know. Your training as a Shadow Lady covers it. What do you feel you need to learn?" His eyes glanced to Avery.

"The whip, Master."

Avery gasped. Why in the hell would Nikki want to do that?

"No. What the fu—" He made a growling sound in the back of his throat. "No." Ryse threw his hands up in the air. He shook his head and huffed around the small square of a stall. "Don't do this. No."

"Master," Nikki bowed her head, "on that day, I died under the whip and I will rise again by the whip."

Ryse's head snapped to her, his features carved in stone. "Are you trying to punish me? Is this payback?"

"Ryse, please," Avery whispered and touched his arm.

"No." Nikki held up her hands. "No, Master. Please don't think that. It's a reminder for me. It's a retribution, of sorts."

"Avery?" Ryse turned, his voice pleading for her support.

She held up her hands in surrender. "I'm not holdin' her back. Might not be my first choice, but..." She outstretched her arms, physically putting distance between her and this decision.

"You're sure about this?" Ryse rubbed his forehead and looked to Nikki.

"Yes."

Ryse grit his teeth. "So be it." He walked away with Nikki trailing behind him, then did an about face and pointed at her. "If this goes wrong, it's on you." Then his shoulders dropped. "Then again, you're not one to shy away from consequences." He narrowed his eyes and huffed off.

Avery almost didn't catch the tiny smile Nikki flashed her.

*I'll hear about this later. I just know it.*

# CHAPTER SIX

## AVERY

THAT AFTERNOON, DYNASTY AND HANNA HAD RETIRED TO THEIR rooms, and Lysandra went to watch Nikki and Ryse train with the whip.

Avery, Yankee, Dante, and Brenden headed to grab food in the kitchens. Avery was hungry as hell and worn out from her lessons. Luckily, so far, nothing had caught on fire again. She kept the guns strapped to her side mainly because it made her feel like an action movie hero. Silly, but for once, she felt powerful and strong with her powers, weapons, and new life. For once, she wasn't a victim anymore. That liberation was beautiful.

If only Frank were here to see it. He would be so proud.

"You're still an asshole," Dante snarled at Yankee, regaining her attention. Yankee flipped him the bird, completely unaffected by the insult.

"Some things never change," she said under her breath.

"You shouldn't mess with her. Lysa knows your crap and half

of everyone else's." Brenden's eyebrows rose high on his forehead. He blew out a deep breath and shook his head. They all looked at him like he was insane.

Lysandra? The Oracle—Oh wait, yeah. She totally understood. Of course these guys didn't want to mess with a woman who could see your past, present, or future with the slightest touch or even a nudge from the gods.

"For real. I'm not playing." Brenden shook his hands in front of him as if wiping away their disbelief. "You always have to watch the quiet ones."

"Just look at Nikki," Yankee said, bringing their entire group to a halt in the foyer of the palace.

"Did you really just say that?" Avery pursed her lips.

Brenden bristled up and stepped chest to chest with Yankee. "What're you getting at?"

Yankee remained completely unresponsive and stared him down. "I'm just agreeing with you."

"No, you're trying to insult my woman. It's not bad enough you nearly split up Dante and Lysa with that hooker—"

"Hooker?" Avery's mouth fell open. "Where? When? What the hell?"

"—now you're trying to cause issues with me and Nikki?"

"Back the fuck up, okay?" Yankee pushed him off. "This is why Thracians shouldn't mate. You idiots lose your minds." He tried to walk away.

"Hold the phones." Avery threw her hands up. "What about the hooker? There are Olympian hookers?"

"Yeah, Avery." Yankee rolled his eyes. "It's divine puss—"

"*Oomph.*"

All four of them turned to see a dark-headed woman sitting in the middle of the foyers as if she'd fallen out of the air. Her chest pumped up and down hard with exertion. Her head swung around, black hair flying. Onyx eyes darted around wildly at the four of them, and her mouth hung wide open.

"Who the hell are you and how'd you get here?" Avery opened her hand and gathered her fire powers focused into a ball in her hand, ready to defend. The three Thracians crouched, ready for a fight.

The girl's body shook, but recognition lit on her face as if she'd just discovered gold.

"You, I need *you*." She reached for Avery.

"Oh hell no." Yankee and Brenden lunged at her at the same moment.

Upon contact, Avery's world twisted and churned. The palace disappeared and everything went black for the blink of an eye.

When her eyes focused again, she stood in the middle of hell, a scene she knew all too well.

*Oh gods, I'm not ready for this again.*

Bodies littered the ground. Blood ran on the floors and gunshots sounded off, their targets' wounds adding to the red river.

Everyone in the room paused when they dropped in. Rogues, wearing the same uniforms as the ones who invaded her home the night Ryse took her away, filled the room. Based on the chairs, the reception desk, and the sterile smell, they'd been taken to a hospital or something.

"What in the blue blazes have you done?" Avery's heart raced in her chest and heat began in her feet and traveled up her legs. Her fire was coming and she didn't want to stop it. Her shoes disintegrated as her feet turned into living flame.

Yankee pulled the black-headed girl behind him. "Where the fuck are we?" he screamed as the Rogues attacked.

It didn't matter.

Avery didn't wait for the answer. The fire heated her knees and her hips and spread into her core, moving rapidly upward towards her hands. Her clothes were instantly gone, along with all the weapons strapped to her side.

*Dang it! Fire balls it is.*

She flung out her arms, sending fire like a blowtorch, taking out three men around her, their bullets whizzing right through her. One hit Brenden's leg and he roared, his inner beast awakened.

His body shifted and contorted into the multi-animal beast he considered his curse from the gods. His body grew massive and covered in thick brown fur. Yellow flooded his eyes, but his face morphed into something resembling a canine. The first time Avery had seen his eagle-like talons, she'd prayed they didn't kill Ryse. Today, she hoped they shredded every Rogue in the place.

The black-headed girl had already disappeared again and moved across the room. She lifted a gun, pulled the trigger, and planted two bullets in some guy's head and then zipped out of sight. She might have needed their help, but she clearly didn't need their protection.

Avery grabbed a man by his gun hand, his eyes round in terror. Her flames rushed down his body, and his screams rang in her ears as she moved on.

Between Avery's fire, Brenden's beast, and Yankee's incredible speed, they took out the Rogues in the hospital. These were not Thracian warriors who could've put up a real fight. They were regular Olympians armed with guns and nothing more. Once they saw who they were fighting, they tried to retreat.

Avery showed no mercy. Retreating Rogues were still Rogues. She threw a ball of orange and red flames at a man running for the door of the clinic. It was the last one she saw standing.

She ducked into one of the offices and calmed down her aura, mentally placing shields around her powers so her flames would retreat. Thank the gods, Nikki's blood was still mixing well with hers, because otherwise, she would've been walking around butt naked. She conjured similar clothing to the ones she'd had on earlier. The textures and feeling of the clothing were familiar enough that it didn't take much effort. She also figured that once Brenden calmed down enough to shift back into a human, he might need clothing as well.

Unfortunately, she didn't know anything about his sizes, so she had to wing this little production line. She exited the office holding a black shirt and a pair of jeans.

"This one was a Thracian, damn it," Yankee said, crouched over a body, checking for a pulse. "I recognize him. He's one that Ryse recently sent up here. We're in Chicago."

"Chicago?" Avery went behind the reception desk and rifled through a stack of papers. *Ralpha Clinic.* It sounded familiar, but nothing clicked immediately.

"This is Ryse's cousin's place." Brenden popped his head out of a room, his bare chest showing. "Um, Avery?"

"Oh, hey, I got this." She threw him the clothes. "How exactly did we get dropped into this mess?"

"She's a teleporter." Yankee rose, his face filthy with the blood of his victims. "Which means we may never see her again."

"But where is Evander?" Brenden came out of the room. "Now we have to find out why these jerks slaughtered innocent civilians in a hospital."

"Maybe they're looking for something?" Avery noticed all the papers strewn about. "This place is trashed. All the records are messed up."

Brenden bent down and checked a woman in scrubs for a pulse. "These were needless murders."

The black-headed girl flashed in, appearing right in the middle of the room where Brenden was. Her eyes rounded and she covered her mouth at the sight of the carnage.

Bren rose to face her. "Are you going to tell us what kind of hell you just dropped us into?"

She might have lifted her chin defiantly, but her voice still shook when she answered. "This is the Ralpha Clinic for Olympians. It's run by—"

"Evander Castille," Yankee butted in. He crossed his arms over his chest and glared at the girl. "We know that. Tell us what we don't know."

"The Rogues invaded and—"

"That's pretty evident."

Yankee's snark apparently wasn't taken well, because the girl rounded on him and poked him in the chest like she had every right to do so. "Will you shut up long enough to let me answer your questions?"

Avery gasped and nearly choked on her laughter. Not too many people had the stones to stand up to Yankee, especially those who just met him.

"Who the hell do you think you are?"

"I'm Keona Nadal," she said, proudly lifting her chin. Yankee blanched, Brenden froze.

Avery had no idea what that meant, but it was enough to silence two of the mouthiest people she knew.

"I'm the daughter of Marlaina Nadal. I met Evander about two months ago and he took us in. My sister is a Divine Grace and she's missing."

Avery grasped her chest. This was who they were looking for! Hayden's Grace had been right there, under Evander's roof.

"Now can we please skip the rest of the introductions and look for Evander and my sister?"

Avery didn't hesitate. If there was even a slim chance of finding Hayden's Grace, they had to quit posturing and get to searching. "Spread out. Brenden, come with me. Yankee, stay with Keona. We'll take the east corridor; you guys search the west." Without even looking back to see if the guys had obeyed, she took off, searching every room. The scene was gruesome. Blood painted the walls with horrific tales of exactly how these unfortunate people spent their last moments. Some were slumped against the walls where they'd been shot and slid right to the floor. Others were crouched in corners, slaughtered needlessly. Some of the rooms told of Olympic magic, maybe used in self-defense, maybe used to kill. One body was charred and Avery had to control the urge to vomit. A man in scrubs was still holding a knife, his attacker dead beneath him.

"Look at the blood on his back," Brenden whispered as if he would disturb the dead. "Those are entrance wounds. He fought off the guy beneath him only to be shot in the back."

"This is worse than my house." Avery shook her head and allowed herself to mourn the loss of life. "These people did nothing wrong. They…they came to us for help and were murdered."

Brenden wrapped his arm around her shoulders. "We'll find who orchestrated this. Don't you worry. It's what I do."

"Do you know what Evander looks like? I was kinda dead when he came to visit." Avery sniffed and wiped her eyes of the tears.

"I do, and none of these people are Evander Castille."

"Avery! Bren!" Yankee yelled down the hall as he came jogging. "She did that disappearing thing again, damn it. She mentioned the safe room. I know where it is. Come on." Yankee grabbed guns off of the bodies of Rogues that littered the clinic.

The men made sure Avery was between them as they exited the building and crossed the open yard to the garages of the Mediterranean-style mansion. The three of them crouched low, checking ahead and behind before every move they made.

Their silence was unnecessary. There wasn't a pulse in the entire place. Avery's heart sank as she heard Keona crying out.

"Come back, please, Evander. Wake up. Please don't go."

Avery pushed past Bren and motioned for him to stay at the door, only to find Keona crouched over a beaten and bloodied body. "Oh no. Is that Evander? Ryse's cousin?" Her cousin, more family members taken before she had the chance to really know them.

Keona's long black hair was matted to her face by her tears. She stroked Evander's head over and over again, right over the slick red blood. "He told me to go. He, he made me leave him. If I would've stayed, I could've protected him. I…I…" Her words dissolved into sobbing and Avery bent down to comfort her. If Evander sent her away, there was a reason.

"This isn't your fault." Avery pushed her hair out of her face and the pain in Keona's eyes said that she disagreed. "The Rogues killed him. Not you. This isn't your fault, okay?"

Keona's whole demeanor changed. She looked at Avery as if she were a savior. "My sister is gone too."

"We have a tracker, Keona. We can find her."

*Dear gods, please let me be tellin' the truth to this poor girl.*

Brenden came in behind her finally. Yankee was on the phone relaying where they were and what happened. Bless his little heart, Brenden spoke softly and kindly as not to spook Keona more. "It's all clear, Avery. There's nothing else alive around here. Yankee is on the phone with Ryse. We need to get you back to the Haven, ASAP."

"Avery? You're the Master Thracian's mate?"

Avery gave her a smile. Even in the midst of all the chaos, she was happy to be known as the Master Thracian's wife. "That'd be me, darlin'."

Keona's anguish began anew, so intense that Avery had a hard time understanding her. "Your husband…kill me for sure."

# CHAPTER SEVEN

## PIPER

PIPER'S HEAD BOUNCED AGAINST THE HARD FLOOR OF THE VEHICLE. She moaned as she came awake with another thud. Even after blinking her eyes open, she couldn't see anything. Some sort of bag covered her head.

"Whatever you do, keep your aura tight," whispered a familiar deep bass. Her body relaxed a fraction.

"Cain?"

"Yes, milady. Keep yourself under control. Do not expose what you are."

*Bang. Bang. Bang.* "Hey, shut the hell up back there," screamed another man from further off, possibly the driver. He banged his fist against the sidewall.

Piper thought of the steel box and she captured her aura mentally, locking it tight behind her mental shields.

"Good girl," Cain whispered beside her. "I can't sense you at all."

*Thunk.* "Ugh." Cain coughed and wheezed.

"I said, shut the hell up, you monster." This time, the other male sounded closer. Not the driver, the passenger. So there were at least two other people in the vehicle—a van, if she had to guess by the way she was able to stretch out. Her hands and feet were bound. Luckily, nothing was over her mouth. Wherever they were headed, her captors didn't care if she screamed, which meant there would be no one around to hear her cries for help.

Her heart pounded in her ears and she tried to control her panic the way her mother had taught her. No one lives if they lose control.

Her body ached, but being tackled by men will do that. None of them had hit her or tried to kill her the way they had done to Nicholas. She would never be able to get that image out of her head. The sword of the enemy emerging from the center of his chest, the way his blood trickled out, then spurted when the sword retracted. She could still feel his weight, as he fell over on her for support, and see the life leave his eyes.

Such a good man, such an asset to the Olympian world, forever gone. It broke her heart.

Piper was a healer. Her sole purpose in this world was to make people better, take away their pain, and make them right again. To watch someone she cared about die in front of her went against everything she believed in.

It was her gut instinct to reach over and heal him. For a split second, she gave it everything she had.

Then she stopped.

Nicholas died because of her. It wouldn't have taken long to heal the knife wound, but she stopped herself. He wasn't dead when she crawled to his body and put her hands on his chest.

She knew better than to reveal herself to the enemy. To use her powers to heal, she had to open her aura. Even the slightest crack would've tipped off her attackers. Keona warned her. Her sister had told her to keep her aura on lockdown and she had.

Nicholas died in her arms, knowing full well that she could've saved him. His blood was on her hands forever.

"I wonder if they'll bring in the Prophet to see this one?" one of the men asked, his voice high and nasally.

"I hope not. That dude freaks me out," answered his counterpart, a man who bore the effects of too much smoking. His voice was raspy and he stank of the habit.

"You've seen him?"

"Yeah, I caught a glance, you know. They keep him locked up tight."

"So, if you've seen him, then answer me this: What is he?"

The van took a corner, pushing her body up against someone else. Cain. "Listen close, Princess." His voice was barely a sound, but she heard him.

"They say he's an experiment gone wrong. He used to be an Olympian, a shape shifter of sorts. He could transform into one of those big lizard things. He didn't like his powers, thought they were useless, and when the chance came to sign up for this experimental program, he was first in line. They injected him with demon blood all over his body, like a weird transfusion thing."

"Doesn't Prince Ashton use demon blood?"

"Yeah, but not like this, though. They nearly replaced all this dude's blood with a demon's. The first time a demon materialized in this realm, everyone was shocked as shit. He didn't last long, though. The second time they called one from Hades, they were smart enough to cut off one of its limbs and keep it."

"You mean to tell me, they pump this guy up with all this demon blood and it turned him into a monster?"

"Oh, he's a certified freak. Part Olympian, part demon, and scary as hell. He bows to Ashton, but that sonofabitch didn't want to take orders from anyone so they locked him up. He got to that girl in Texas, the one that's mated to the Master Thracian. They say he has a taste for flesh."

"Gross."

"Go tell him that."

A cell phone went off, a horrible 80s song for the ring tone. "Yes, sir?"

Piper couldn't hear the whole conversation, but she picked up on one word: *teleporter*.

"Do you know where we're going?" Piper whispered so softly that sound barely escaped her mouth. If the men were distracted by a phone call, maybe she could get some answers.

Cain would hear; his Thracian senses picked up on everything. "No."

"How did they catch you?"

"I let them."

"Why?" She almost screamed at him. If her legs weren't bound, she would've kicked him for being foolish.

"I knew they'd caught you."

Her heart nearly shattered. "They'll kill you, Cain, or worse."

"Then I shall die doing my damnedest to protect you."

Piper cried again. He'd doomed himself for her, Nicholas had died because of her; who else would pay the price of her existence? What about her sister? Where was Keona? What had Ashton done to her that she couldn't telepathically connect to her sister? They'd always had a bond as twins, no matter the distance or circumstances.

The thought of Keona being dead had her entire body shaking with fear. *No, I would feel it. I would know.* Had she gone to the Haven? Had Ashton found her too? Had she and Evander escaped somehow?

The van sailed over a bump and sent Piper crashing into Cain, their heads colliding.

"Ugh," Cain groaned, and the warm copper scent of blood hit her nose.

"Sorry," she whispered.

"It's okay, you're closer now." He leaned forward until she could feel his head right next to hers through the bags. "No matter what happens to me, you keep that aura of yours closed. Don't heal, don't let down your guard, and no matter what they do to me, you keep your mouth shut. Do you understand?"

"Yes."

"You're a Divine Grace. Once Ashton knows that, he will want you for himself. You do what it takes to get out in public, then make a scene, use your powers, something the Castilles' tracker will notice."

"Why? They hate my family."

"Hayden Castille is your Prince, the man who visits you in your dreams. Keona confirmed my suspicions. You do what it takes to make sure Ashton gets you in public and you draw attention. They will come for you."

The van came to a stop and Piper held her breath. Would they separate her from Cain? Would they kill him? They started driving again.

"I'm scared."

"I know, Princess. Fear not. The gods will protect you if I cannot. We may be traveling a distance. Rest while you can."

Rest? *Rest?* Was he insane? They were being kidnapped and he wanted her to take a nap?

Unfortunately, Cain was right. Piper's body ached as they drove and drove. She needed to use the bathroom, but she controlled her body's response and made her bladder calm down.

"He said we have to cross here at this time," said the guy with the high-pitched voice after hours of silence.

"You sure?"

"Yeah. He texted me the location and which way to go through."

Cross? Go through? Where were they going? Were they crossing the border into Canada? Mexico? She didn't know which direction they were heading. Who was guiding them? It had to be Ashton Avondale.

"Are you sure about this, man?"

"Look, stop being a baby. They said it would be taken care of."

Piper snuggled closer to Cain. "Should I scream?"

"No."

"Why not?"

"It won't matter."

For the first time in her life, she was without her sister, without her guardian. Cain might have been right beside her, but she was truly alone. To keep her aura under control meant no mental communication with her twin.

She hung on to the only ray of hope she had in this situation.

*Hayden.*

*Hayden.*

*Hayden.*

# CHAPTER EIGHT

## AVERY

AVERY HELD HER BREATH AS KEONA EXPLAINED TO RYSE EXACTLY who she was and what she was doing at Evander's compound. The undeniable fear of Ryse was a cloud that hung in the room.

Her mate didn't move as Keona spoke. He stared at Evander's body, motionless and silent, like a tiger ready to strike at its prey.

"I tried to save him." Keona's voice quivered with each word as she clung to the man she loved, now gone from this world.

Evander was another Castille casualty. Avery had no doubt that the Avondales were behind this, or at least Ashton. But how did they prove it?

Avery didn't know much about murder investigations, but she knew to start at the scene of the crime. Each moment they stood there talking to Ryse, explaining it all out, they lost precious time.

This girl was telling the truth. That was all Avery needed to know. She recognized a woman in love and in pain at the loss of that love. There was another Grace out there in danger and this girl was the key to finding her.

As a group of Elites and Thracians prepared to go back to Evander's estate, Avery glanced down at Brenden's leg. It was bandaged up, but blood was still soaking the cloth.

"You need to stay here, Bren. You're hurt."

"Just a flesh wound." He brushed her off. "Besides, where you go, I go. And I'm kinda the lead investigator of the Thracians."

"Really?" Was he pulling her leg or was he for real? She never really knew with Bren.

"How'd we meet, Avery? Think about it." He winked and elbowed her.

The first time she'd met Bren, he'd come into her café as a police officer. "Oh," she said to herself. Of course Brenden was a trained officer; he'd been under cover for months before all hell broke loose in her hometown. Thracians were placed in every position of human law enforcement from traffic cops to the CIA and FBI. With Brenden's animal instincts, he surely made one hell of an investigator.

The group that was going back to Chicago circled and Brenden started giving out orders. All of the Elites and a handful of Thracian soldiers were at the ready.

"Listen up," Brenden barked. "I'll lead group one through the house, where our primary victim was found. With me are Avery, Keona, Dante, and you three." He pointed at a group of men Avery had never seen before.

Dante raised his fingers in the air. "I'm afraid if the method of travel is based on teleportation," he sucked in a breath, "I won't be able to go."

Avery sighed as, one by one, people caught on.

"Why not?" Keona asked. "I can take multiple people."

Dante touched her shoulder. "Try to go."

Keona's body jerked once, twice, three times before she backed away from Dante with wide, frightened eyes, her hands in front of her defensively. "Holy shit, man." She glanced at the people standing around. Her body shivered. "What the hell was that?"

"I cancel out Olympian powers." Dante lifted his tensed jaw, but Avery could see the sting of rejection in his eyes.

"Dante is also a shield from attacks." She stepped up in his defense. "He's saved my life."

"Yeah, that's great, but don't take it personally if I keep my distance."

Dante's lips went tight. "You wouldn't be the first."

Brenden clapped his hands together, taking the focus off of Dante. "Okay, Dante will be our contact here at base. If you need backup, he's the man to call. He can relay with Keona. Hammon, you're incident commander for group two, who will be in the clinic. Cutter will join you and the four of you will assist."

That group sectioned themselves off.

Brenden pointed to his left. "Yankee, group three commander. Philippe will assist, and since this is in a park, I need you." He studied the remaining soldiers. "You, and you in civilian clothes in two minutes. Nikki will provide you with those. Go in there." He sent the men off with Nikki to a nearby office area where they could change. "The rest of you guys are on exterior patrol and recon. The compound covers about ten acres and we need every shred of information we can get. I want to know how these Rogues got past the guards, I want a head count of every Thracian soldier there and where they should've been during their watch.

"We have a high body count, which means this is not going to be a quick in and out. I want pictures of everything before you touch anything. I want patient logs from the clinic and matching bodies. If there is so much as a janitor who's missing, there but shouldn't be, or should be but isn't, I want to know about it."

"Plan of entry?" Yankee asked.

"Keona will take team three to the park first, exterior recon team second, team two will be third, and once the mansion is secured, team one will enter."

"And she can do all that?" Yankee's eyes traveled up and down Keona, who all but snarled at him.

She cocked out one hip and crossed her arms over her chest, glaring back. "Yeah, I can do *that* and more."

Before they could tear into each other, the other Thracians and Nikki returned. One came back dressed as a runner, one a businessman, and another wearing jeans and a baseball cap. Even in their "civilian clothes," the three of them looked like wrestlers.

Nikki came to stand right behind Avery. "Wherever you go, I go."

Avery nodded once. "Can you handle this? It's ugly. Trust me."

"Wherever you go, I go." Nikki swallowed hard and kept her stance firm, her eyes focused away from Avery's. Gone was the soft and sweet woman Avery had come to love. What remained of Nikki was hard and determined. It hurt to see the drastic change in her friend, but there was no going back, and both of them had to come to terms with who Nikki was now.

All the men checked their phones and various communication devices. The different teams all had cameras and bags full of tools used for gathering evidence.

"Got your man purse?" Keona asked as she stuck her hand out to Yankee, who threw the satchel over his shoulder.

He sneered at her and took her hand.

"I have to make contact with those I'm transporting, so hang on." The guys in Yankee's team all grabbed on to her arm or shoulder and once she double-checked that she had everyone, she disappeared.

"That is freakin' cool." Avery grinned at Nikki.

"Her gift is her greatest asset and her greatest liability." Dante's sand-colored eyes met hers. "She is hunted, and I have no doubt her existence is what led to the massive loss of life at the compound."

Avery tilted her head to the side. "You say that like you hold her responsible."

"I can't make that call. But if she was using her gifts in the open, a power like that would've caught the attention of every Olympian nearby. If she's really Marlaina Nadal's child," he shrugged his round shoulders and crinkled his nose, "she should know better."

About that time, Keona returned and locked hands with the recon group. She tipped her head to Brenden and, *poof,* she was gone.

"Did you feel that?" Dante asked the two women.

Nikki and Avery both shook their heads. What did they miss?

"She knows how to shield her aura, which means she should've known her powers are like a radar to trackers."

Avery shook her head again. "Well, you don't know what you don't know, you know?"

Dante and Nikki both looked at her with blank expressions.

"That must be a southern-ism." Dante rubbed his forehead.

"It is," Brenden and Avery answered in unison and then exchanged grins. Both of them came from Texas and they understood the little sayings and spoke the same language.

Keona dispatched team two with the same speed and efficiency as the others. Once Hammon called with the green light, Keona reached out a hand to Avery.

"You ready?"

"Oh, *now* you ask me? That's like closin' the barn door *after* the horses are out." Avery rolled her eyes dramatically.

Keona's lips pulled back into a shy smile. "You're going to be trouble, I can tell."

"You betcha, girl." She winked at Dante, whose tense shoulders and flared nostrils signaled his displeasure with not being able to go with her. "I'll be careful." Avery held Keona's hand and, once again, the world flipped inside out and upside down as she transported them back to the compound.

The stench of blood hit hard, knocking the air out her lungs.

"Oh, god." She closed her eyes and covered her mouth, trying to get control of her gag reflexes.

"If you need to leave, go," Brenden said, his voice laced with concern. "You don't have to be here, Avery."

She waved him off. "No, no. I want to help. I need to learn. It's, uh, just a strong odor. I'm fine, really."

Nikki and Avery both observed as Brenden went over the crime scene. The other men did exactly what they were told. Every minute detail was photographed, catalogued, and numbered.

Keona was essential to helping identify clinic staff, household staff, and showing the investigators how she remembered things.

"What will you do with all the bodies?" She looked to Brenden, her dark eyes full of unshed tears and her voice quiet.

"We've already called in a local team for cleanup. The humans will never know what happened here and the Olympians will all be identified and investigated along with everyone they are linked to. Don't worry." Bren gave her a tight smile. "We have a lot more troops than you think." He cleared the main part of the house and then went to the master suite. "Can you handle this?"

Keona glanced to Avery, then nodded. "I promised Prince Hayden I would come back quickly. But Evander will need something to wear for…" She glanced up at the ceiling, blinking back the tears. Keona bit her trembling bottom lip and gnawed on it until she could speak again.

"It's okay." Avery took her hand and put an arm around her, giving her strength and support. "I'll help."

Keona didn't speak, just nodded fast and led the way into the master closet to pick out the last change of clothes Evander would ever wear. She knew exactly what he preferred, right down to the socks.

Seeing Keona lovingly petting Evander's dress shirt broke Avery's heart. She couldn't imagine losing Ryse, even after the short time they'd been together; her entire life would fall apart without him.

He was her reason for waking in the morning and the reason she could sleep at night. If Keona had found even a fraction of that love with Evander, the loss would be devastating.

"Keona, who is this?" Brenden was crouched over a woman holding a child. She'd been shot in the back of the head.

"That's, oh god, that's Evander's maid." She closed her eyes and blew out a breath. "Her name is Sylvie, and if I'm not mistaken, that's her son, but he didn't come around much."

"This boy didn't die here." Brenden called over several of his men to examine the pair. He stood up and talked to Avery and Keona. "Most of these bodies are in the very beginning stages of rigor. They're still fresh; the settling of the blood is still happening. This boy is in the final stages of rigor and has obvious lividity, which means he's been dead much longer."

"How can you tell?" Avery, unfortunately, only saw a dead child and nothing more with her untrained eyes.

"When the blood settles after death, it turns the skin purple, except where something was pushing on it. See how the boy has these striations on his arms? That means when he died, he lay against something with ridges."

"What would make those?"

Brenden put his hands on his hips and shook his head. "I won't know until we can get the body in for processing. But if I had to guess, these two right here are the answer to a lot of questions."

Since Avery had nothing but questions, she hoped Brenden, with all this training, had some answers.

The men took care to take pictures and examine everything around the bodies curled up together.

"Yeah, this boy didn't die on this surface." Brenden touched the boy's arm. "Hell, he's not even warm."

"What are you thinking?" Nikki bent down and placed her gloved hand on the boy just like Bren did.

"Someone moved his body here to make him look like a victim of the raid. You said he was hardly ever here?" Bren eyed Keona.

"In the last couple months, I've seen him twice, maybe three times, when she came in to get her paycheck."

Brenden bent down even closer to the little black-haired boy and sniffed him. Then he sniffed Sylvie, the mom. "Two different scents. I can tell they are family, but he has been in a different location for a while. His scent is off."

"I don't smell anything but blood." Nikki inhaled deeply and coughed.

"That's because I'm part wolf and you're part angel." He touched her chin and winked.

Nikki shook her head and stood.

"Okay, I'm going to stay here for a bit and keep looking. Avery, Nikki, you need to get back to the Haven. Keona?"

She had gone over to Evander's desk and picked up a picture frame. Tears trickled down her face. Avery wanted desperately to relieve her of her pain, but that was far beyond her skills.

The two faces in the picture smiled at the camera, so in love and happy. Evander and Keona had magic together and it was evident even in a photograph.

"We were right here in this office," she whispered. "He said he needed a picture of me to put on his desk." She sniffed and wiped her nose. "He hated the fact that it was a selfie, but it was something he could print here." She handed Avery the picture.

Avery held it up to get better light and realized she was facing the wall behind them in the picture. A black hole in the books on the wall wasn't there in the picture. Her eyes flickered to the bookshelf, the picture, the bookshelf, the picture. "There's a title missing." She approached the library wall and pointed it out to Brenden. "Look, this book was right here and now it's gone."

"Books are thrown everywhere. How do you know it's not on the floor somewhere?" Nikki bent to pick up a book.

"Don't touch, please." One of the Thracians with a camera came over and snapped a bunch of pictures.

Brenden's cell phone rang, interrupting the clicking and mumbles. "Sir? Yes, right now, okay." He pointed at Avery. "Sending her now."

Avery rolled her eyes. "Fine, fine, I'm goin'. I might've just cracked the case, but I can't be unattended for five minutes."

"You do tend to get yourself killed," Nikki said softly, receiving a side glare. "Sorry."

Avery cleared her throat and held out her hands. She focused on the weight of the picture, the components like the wooden frame, the glass cover, the colors of the picture. Keona wiped her eyes when Avery handed her the replica. "Can't take the original, but this one's all yours, sister."

"Thank you." Keona tried so hard to be strong. She really did. The effort was valiant, but Avery wanted her to feel free to be vulnerable in front of her. One day, they would be family. In the eyes of the gods, they already were.

Avery cringed when she thought about what had happened to her first conjuring experiment. "Oh, um, be careful because that might catch on fire."

# CHAPTER NINE

## LYSANDRA

S HE SWALLOWED THE LUMP IN HER THROAT AND ENTERED THE LIBRARY of the Thracian Training Center. Lysandra sought out Dante after she heard that Avery was gone and he was still at the palace. That was not a good sign.

After a thousand years of living as an Oracle in the City of Delphi, never being around men, walking into a building dominated by testosterone-fueled men was like walking onto a foreign planet.

"May I help you find your way, milady?" A mountain of a man bent at the waist and bowed his head to her. "My name is Platon. I oversee the men here."

Lysandra kept her chin up and shoulders squared. "My name is—"

"Lady Lysandra, the Oracle from Delphi. It is an honor to have you visit us." He smiled, and she got the feeling the action wasn't natural for him.

"I am looking for the Elite apprentice, Dante. I believe he was seen heading this direction."

The corner of his mouth turned down and he scratched his chin. "If I'm not mistaken, he did come in. I believe you can find him in the stables. May I escort you?" He offered her his arm, which was the size of a tree trunk.

"Thank you, Thracian."

"How are you liking the Haven?" Platon asked as they exited the back of the building. Soldiers were littered about the area and all stopped to stare at her. When these men gazed upon her, it was easy to ignore. There was only one man whose eyes she desired.

"It is beautiful, thank you."

"I have a personal inquiry, if you will permit it."

"Certainly." She kept walking, her eyes remaining straight ahead as they went through the second building labeled as the dormitories.

"Is it true that you summoned the god Apollo, that he might heal my brother, Dante, and that you have chosen to become his mate?"

"I did and I have. Is that a problem for you, Platon?"

"No, milady."

"Then why do you ask?"

"Because Dante is a good man and a good Thracian. He is lucky to have the favor of the gods and you." He held out his hand towards a field. There was a path by the fence leading to a long metal building.

"Do Thracians often work with animals? I didn't know this was common practice."

"We have certain men with affinities for animals. You will see." Platon bowed low again. "Good day to you, milady."

"And you." Lysandra's heart thudded in her chest as she approached the barn and heard Dante's low, rumbling laugh. Everything about him made her senses come alive.

He was leaned up against the stall door, his elbows resting on the top, his voice directed at whoever was in the stall. "…it's just working against me again, you know?"

"Trust me, I get it, man. Gifts like ours, they have drawbacks. But that doesn't make them any less important. Besides, you're a guardian of the Master's mate. How cool is that?"

Lysandra cleared her throat. Dante's head turned and a smile blossomed over his face.

His open affection made her stomach flutter. "I'm sorry to interrupt."

"No, no, it's fine." He held out a hand and then pulled her close to his side. "Lysa, I'd like you to meet my friend, Ixion."

The young man in the stall rose up and up and up. He was gigantic, even for a Thracian. "The Oracle." He bowed and, even folded in half, was nearly as tall as she was. He was dark headed and had a youthful face. "It's a pleasure to meet you. Dante doesn't shut up about you."

"Watch it," Dante growled, his cheeks taking on a blush.

"I hope it's all positive. Are you one of the men with the gift of animals?"

"I am." He stood straight with his hands behind his back. His nervousness was endearing. "Would you like to see?"

"Yes." She allowed Dante to lead her to the middle of the walkway between the rows of stalls.

Ixion exited the horse stall, bending his head to go through the door. "There are two stables in this Haven. One belongs to the royal family; this one is the Thracians'. We have many creatures here." He held up a hand. "Come out, guys."

Four stall doors opened and four horses came out into the walkway. Lysandra gasped. "Oh!"

He introduced her to each of them and each of them bowed, extending their front right legs. The majestic animals delighted her, and she laughed. "Hello."

More creatures came out. Dogs sat in between horses, cats prowled the doors, birds flew overhead, and one landed on Ixion's finger.

Lysandra's delight could not be contained. "How very blessed you are indeed!" She laughed and picked up one of the cats.

A vision came over her. This one felt odd, strange, as if the mind was not completely formed. The perspective was off. Everything was much taller than in her normal view and it took her a moment to realize that this was from the eyes of the cat. The little one had heard Dante's entire story and recalled the memory to her.

Lysandra blinked and saw Ixion staring at her.

"What did you see?" Dante asked.

She buried her face in the soft fur of the cat and kissed its head. "Apparently, your animals listen well. They understand what you're saying, so I would not question the gods' gifts in front of them." The cat hopped from Lysa to Dante and he scrambled to catch it. "She was telling on you, I believe."

Dante held up the creature to look it in the eyes. "Tattle-tale."

All the animals gathered around Ixion. Two more Thracians came into the stables and Lysandra took a step towards Dante, inconspicuously taking him by the hand. The simple act drained her powers, but by now, she was used to it.

The men were not as kind looking as Ixion and even the animals shied away. These men were much older and their eyes held the tales of war and battle, something young Ixion didn't have.

One, with a dark complexion and dark brown eyes, stared at her. "I didn't think women were allowed back here."

"Platon escorted her himself." Ixion waved his hand and sent all the animals away, all but a certain cat.

"My apologies," said the man with dark eyes. "Are you certain you're in the right place, milady? Not too many visitors come to see the animals. There are more impressive things to study."

"Perhaps you would like a personal tour," offered the other man, who wore a baseball cap.

Lysa squeezed Dante's hand when he stepped forward to defend her. "Actually, gentlemen, I'm here on behalf of the Master Thracian's mate. She requires Dante and Ixion's presence."

"*Them?*" The two guys looked at each other, scoffing.

"Absolutely. These men were handpicked by the Lady. What do you do again?"

The three of them laughed all the way to the palace, the cat in tow. Before they entered, Ixion stopped and gazed up at the ornate door. "I've never been in here before," he said as he lifted his eyes up and up and up to the top of the castle.

The large door opened and there stood Lady Dynasty, Hanna at her side. "That makes me a poor hostess."

Ixion dropped to his knee. "My Queen."

"Rise, Thracian, and be welcomed in my home…along with your friends." Her lavender eyes lit and she smiled.

They turned to see two cats and a dog peeking out from behind the water fountain.

"I'm sorry, my Queen. I told them to—"

"Not another word. All creatures great and small are welcome here. Will you join us for dinner? I believe Avery is cooking."

"Y-yes, it would be an honor." Ixion's eyes widened and he bent to follow them inside.

"Tell me about yourself, Ixion." Dynasty took him by the arm and Lysandra by the hand. The connection sent her into a vision, which was planned, no doubt about it.

*Dogs sniff the ground, the air, the walls; searching. Cats crawl into tiny crevices and act as spies. Birds flock above a building, indicating there is someone special inside.*

*A blonde woman cowers in a corner, crying, while a man tries to speak softly to her. No matter what he says, he can't be trusted. No one will help her now.*

*The woman's hair changes color to midnight black. She's curled up in a bed, crying, waiting for someone to rescue her. No matter what he says, he can't be trusted. Who will help her now?*

Lysa shook off the fog of her vision and now that the information had been transferred, Dynasty let her hand go. She stepped back to link arms with Dante.

"Your friend is important to our search," she whispered as a cat ran between them to walk next to Ixion.

"Vision?"

"Yes."

"I wish you could have visions while touching me. I'm sorry."

Lysa pulled him into a hallway and let the others keep going. "Kiss me."

Dante didn't hesitate. He wrapped both arms around her and pressed his mouth to hers. Immediately, she opened her mouth to him, her body tingling as his tongue brushed against hers. Her heart thudded in her chest and she heated up from the inside out.

When he pulled back, they were both breathing hard. His eyes held a wildness that only made her hotter. She slid her hands over his chest and up his neck. "When I touch you, my mind is cleared. My thoughts are on you alone. I don't have to be worried that I will have a vision at an inopportune moment, or that it will interrupt our kisses. You are my focus. You are all I see. I think the gods knew what they were doing when they sent me here to you. I need that relief, and you need my appreciation of your gift."

He closed his eyes and leaned his forehead against hers. "This is why I'm in love with you."

"I love you too, my brave warrior."

"Will you sleep with me again tonight?"

"Are you ill?" Lysandra felt his forehead.

"I can be, if it means getting to curl around you again at night and waking with you in the morning."

Gods, but she loved him, her gentle giant. "Yes, always."

They joined the rest of their companions in the large kitchen and eat-in dining area. All of what she considered their core group was there. The royal family: Dynasty, Hayden, Ryse, and Avery. Their entourage: Nikki, Hanna, Dante, and herself. The Elites: Hammon, Cutter, Philippe, Yankee, and Brenden. General Falcon and the royal guards: Gabrele and Titus.

This was the council of people who commanded the Olympian nation and the Thracians around the world. This was the group of people who trusted each other with their lives.

Tonight, they added two people to the fold. Keona, soon-to-be sister of the Prince, and Ixion, the man who would help save others by way of animals.

Their core was growing larger and stronger.

The mood in the kitchen, however, was somber and fairly quiet. No joking or teasing. Dynasty and Hanna joined Avery and Nikki in the kitchen to finish cooking. Lysa knew nothing about cooking, so she chose to stay with Dante and join the others around the various tables in the breakfast room.

Ryse's face was hard as he leaned back in his chair, arms crossed over his chest, and listened to everything Brenden had to say about their investigation thus far.

"The boy's body was in a van long enough to leave an imprint on his skin. We have our team working out the vehicle's make and model so we can look at surveillance and traffic cameras in the area."

"Cameras at the house?" Ryse asked, his face unyielding.

"Evander's computer was taken. They left the mouse and cords. The video recording server was smashed and burned. There were drag marks in the bathroom that led to the safe room. It looks like Evander—" Brenden glanced over at Keona, whose fists were balled up on the table. "Um, it looks as though the victim was attacked in the bedroom and dragged into the bathroom to open the safe room, then left.

"The books were all accounted for except the one in the picture that Avery noticed. Get this; it's a book on black magic, blood magic. It's written by none other than your favorite witch."

"I thought all her books were destroyed?" Hammon leaned over the table, his black eyes narrowing on Brenden.

"Evander was a scientist," Hayden answered. "Like me, he has rare books that hold information too valuable to lose."

"And too dangerous to be in the hands of Rogues."

Ryse rubbed his temple. "Hammon, you know what this means."

"I will gather my things." He pushed his chair back and stood.

"Nope, sit your butt down." Avery, Nikki, Dynasty, and Hanna all came out of the kitchen with huge trays of food. "Everyone had a crappy day. We're gonna sit here and eat together and visit and rest, you hear me?"

"Man, you came back from the dead all bossy and shit." Yankee picked a steak off the tray of meat. His comment had Ixion's eyes darting between the two of them. Lysandra doubted he'd ever heard a soldier be so informal to a Lady.

"That's what happens when the god of fire wrangles with you." She blew out a heavy breath.

Cutter passed around a plate. He whipped out one of his many hidden knives and speared a potato. "Avery cook in kitchen, and she cook in battle. I find bodies well done today. Some medium rare." He pointed at her with a fork. "I not ever make you mad," he said in broken English.

Lysandra laughed, then covered her mouth to hide it, which only gained the attention of everyone at the table. "I'm sorry. That was in poor taste. I've never heard him make a joke." She shrugged a shoulder, feeling the heat rising in her cheeks.

Cutter met her eyes, his face completely devoid of emotion or expression. "I very funny. What you talking 'bout?"

Brenden and Yankee were the first to start laughing. Avery followed, and before long, even Ryse had a smile on his lips. They passed the food, filled their glasses, and Ryse stood to offer prayer and a toast to Evander Castille.

"To my cousin, my friend, and one damn good man. To the

woman he loved, the clinic he gave his life for, and the gods he served." All of them raised a glass. "May he find rest in the land of the gods."

"May he find rest in the land of the gods."

They ate their meal together, not in silence, but in a quiet respect for Keona and the family. When they were finished, all remained to go over the plans for the next few days.

"Mother," Ryse began, "I want you to help Hayden find a place of deep sleep. If Piper can only reach him in sleep, we need him ready to receive her."

"So you want me in a coma?" Hayden raised a brow.

"Yes." His answer was matter of fact, serious, and without room for argument. "If there is any chance that Piper might reach you, we need to be ready. Mother can help by monitoring your consciousness. Keona, how far can you teleport?"

"Anywhere you need to go."

"Wonderful. How many people can you take?"

She pursed her lips, thinking. "I've moved upwards of ten at a time; never really had to move more."

"Are you joining us?" Ryse's eyes stayed unwavering on her.

"I'm here to find my sister."

"That's not what I asked. Are you with us?"

Keona pointed at Hayden with her glass. "That man is my sister's mate. You might regret it later, but you're pretty much stuck with me. Where my sister stays, I stay."

"Good. I'm assigning you to the Elite guard under the direct service of my wife."

"Wait, you're what?" Keona's brows hit her hairline and her mouth hung open. "Um, not to question your judgment, because I know I'm awesome, but you don't know me. Why would you want to assign me to your wife's guard?"

"Before your mother, and her mother before her, the Nadals and the Castilles were the closest of allies. Your mother worked for my father and for me on several occasions. She was a proud woman, much like you. She knew her worth and knew how to take care of her family with the skills that the gods gave her. I knew your mother. I knew her devotion to her husband and her people. I also know that she traded her life for yours. She did things no god-fearing Olympian should have to because evil people forced her to. Granted, I didn't know she had daughters. That was much later in her life, after she retired, for lack of a better term." Ryse raised his chin and folded his hands in his lap. "You are your mother's daughter. She was fierce, confident, slightly rebellious against authority, and damn good at what she did. More than anything, she was loyal. You've done well, keeping yourself and your sister off the Olympian radar. Hammon hasn't found you and that's a bloody miracle."

"What are you saying?" Keona's jaws were clenched tight.

"You have skills. Evander told me about you fighting off a Thracian. You laid Tomar on his ass, if I was told correctly, and he's not a little man."

"The bigger they are…" Keona brushed it off.

"Exactly. We need your skills. The witch is in London. Hammon and I need to visit her. We don't want to take a plane, if you catch my drift. The sooner we have information from her—"

"The sooner we can find out where my sister is. Got it."

"The fact is," Hammon said, "we are all family here." He motioned around the table and the room. "Avery is not only my master's wife, she is my sister in the gods. Lady Dynasty is not only my queen, but she is my friend, my sister, my family. These are all my brothers here, including my Prince." He pointed a long black hand to Hayden. "Anyone who mates Hayden is my family. I fight for your sister, I fight for you. You fight for your sister, you fight for me."

"I understand." She swallowed and took a deep breath. "And it's a nice sentiment. I'll do whatever it takes to get Piper back, but I'm not used to having people I can depend on. Evander was the first person I've ever trusted besides my sister. I've spent my entire adult life believing this man," she pointed to Ryse, "would kill me on the spot because my mother was labeled a traitor by royals and Thracians around the globe. It's going to take time for that to wear off, you know?"

Avery reached over the table and took Keona's hand. "Trust is earned and it goes both ways. We all accept that. I'm mated to a scary sumbitch. You get used to it."

Ryse rolled his eyes but grinned at Avery.

Lysandra finally spoke up, feeling the gods urge her to speak. "The first time I walked into the palace, I was not exactly welcomed." She gave Yankee a glare.

"Oh, come on, Eight Ball, you were a stranger and you were fucking naked, okay? Give me some mercy here."

"Naked?"

"What?"

"She was naked?"

Keona covered her laughter with her glass, and Lysandra held up her hands to quiet everyone. "I wasn't naked. I had on a cloak. You were a dreadful beast and some things will never change."

"Amen, sister," Avery said around a mouth full of steak. There was a chorus of affirmations, a couple in other languages, along with "Got that right" and "True that."

"My point is, it took me a long time to understand the gods' plan for me and my purpose here. They removed me from the familiar and placed me in the unfamiliar. I won't say it has all been comfortable or easy. It took me a long time to be able to even speak to men, much less care for them." She smiled at Dante, her love, sitting beside her. "You too will have your purpose and destiny revealed with time. Don't be afraid."

"I'm not afraid," Keona said quickly. "I'm a lot of things, sad and worried most of all, but I'm not afraid." Keona stood and smoothed down her shirt. "I can leave for London as soon as you're ready, Master Ryse. But if you don't mind, I need to be alone until then."

Ryse glanced at his watch. "Be in the lobby in two hours."

"Yes, sir." Keona left the breakfast room without another word. Her exodus started the trickle of people going back to the investigation or rest. Ixion was offered a room in the palace, but insisted that he take the animals back to the stables. Cutter thought it would be beneficial to work the dogs around the evidence and see what they could find.

"I can tell them what to do," she overheard Ixion explain, "and I've learned their basic brain functions as far as what they feel and mean. It's not like mind reading, not in the human sense, but if they were to find something that made them upset, I would know. I'd like to work the case, if that's okay?"

"You work with me. Okay. Yes. Tomorrow morning, yes."

Ixion gave Dante a smile-filled thumbs-up as he left the palace with all his creatures in tow.

Dante and Lysandra went back to his room, which she had come to think of as *their* room. "He's a unique person. I like him."

"He was my only friend for a long time." Dante took off his shirt without thinking and threw it in the laundry hamper. He kept talking about Ixion and their friendship, but Lysandra's focus was on his body.

The smooth skin of his shoulders, the line of his neck, the bulges of muscles in his back and arms, the roundness of his behind. Heat coursed through her veins and she pressed her thighs together. Her breasts were too tight in her blouse and they rubbed the fabric with every deep breath.

"Lysa?" He turned around and caught her staring at his bottom. A cocky yet sexy grin played on his lips.

"Sorry." She sat in a chair and pulled off her shoes. Her long black braid fell over her shoulder, only to be picked up by Dante.

"What are you sorry for?" He took her hand and she stood. He was so warm, so clean and fresh smelling, so close.

"I should've been listening to your words. When a man speaks, his woman should listen. I'm sorry."

"No, I like the way you were looking at me."

Heat hit her cheeks like a bright flame on her skin. "You have no idea how I desire you. It scares me sometimes."

"Why would that scare you? It thrills me." His hands went to her hips and she circled his neck, petting the back of his head and the soft blond hair.

"I...I don't..." She shook her head, trying to find the words. "Sometimes when I look at you, I want to know you more, deeper, more intimately. I don't want to take things slow, even though I know we should. You might not want to, you might not always want me—"

"Always, Lysa. I want you always."

"If you change your mind—"

"No. Never. Do you hear me?" He cupped her cheek and met her eyes. "I'll marry you right now, tonight, if that's what it takes to prove how much I love you. Hammon can do it. I'm not picky. But you will be mine for all eternity and I will be yours."

Heaven itself was not as beautiful as those words and the truth behind them.

"You would bind yourself to me? Tonight?"

"Yes. Right now."

Love, rich and wild, exploded and happiness shot off like firecrackers in her heart. She jumped into his arms and wrapped her legs around his waist, planting her lips on his. Nothing could compare to the happiness and joy radiating through her. *He loves me, truly loves me.*

Dante sat on the bed, still holding on to her, kissing her with gusto. Her hands roamed the ridges and mounds of his chest and stomach until she touched the scar in the middle of his stomach. It was hot, almost feverish. Lysandra leaned back and looked into his eyes.

They were black.

"Dante," she gasped. "Your eyes." She backed away and a vision hit her.

*"I can sssee you, pretty little Oracle." The beast laughed at her. "The clossser you get to him, the clossser you get to me. I'll feassst on your flesssh sssoon enough, Lysssandra."*

She covered her mouth to contain her scream. Lysandra shook her head and tears blurred her vision. "You're linked to it. It can see things through you. It saw me."

Dante's eyes had already returned to their sand color, but he backed away, putting distance between them. "I'm not safe, Lysa. You shouldn't be around me."

"No, no, wait. Let me think." Her bottom hit a chair and she sank down in it. "You are linked to the beast, and it comes out when you are most…excited."

"Proving my point; you need to stay away."

"No, I don't." She gazed up at him. "I saw it, Dante. I saw it in a room, a building. I can help locate it—"

"You will go nowhere near it or me again, Lysandra." He grabbed his shirt from the hamper and slipped it on. "I won't risk you."

"He can't touch me." The realization hit her like a ton of bricks. "I'm of the blood of Apollo. I've been bound to the god for centuries. Demons cannot hurt me."

"What are you talking about?" Dante sat back on the bed in front of her.

"Oracles are…neutral." She struggled for the right words. "Our gifts are not biased or loyal to either good or evil. The Pythia sees all, knows all. Even Hades heeds our neutrality. Forces of good and evil alike must not harm an Oracle."

"What makes you think anything demonic or Rogue will care about agreements between gods?"

"It's not just an agreement; it's a blood oath. He can't hurt me any more than you could."

Dante ran his hands through his hair. "I don't think I like where this is headed."

"If I can figure out where he is, why not try?"

"Because I don't want you *exciting* me just so you can gamble on a demon having a conscience." He paced the room, his hands on his waist.

"Maybe it's not just arousal that triggers it." She drummed her fingers on her lips, her mind racing with the possibilities. If she could connect to the demon, maybe she could get a picture of where he was. If they captured the Prophet, it would be a huge victory for Olympians and Thracians worldwide.

"Can we please stop talking about our sexual relationship as if it's a science project?" He rubbed his temple and leaned an elbow on a tall dresser.

"I'm sorry, my warrior." She rose to touch him, but he flinched and shied away.

Lysa gasped. Dante couldn't meet her eyes and he backed off with each advance she made, raising his hands to keep her away.

Lysandra's chest tightened with pain. "Stop it. Don't do that." Her bottom lip trembled. Would he never allow her to touch him again?

"It's not safe for you. *I'm* not safe for you." Dante made for the door.

"What are you doing?" She couldn't breathe. What did she do? How did she keep him with her?

"I won't be a risk to you. I love you too much."

"Show me, then."

He stopped with his hand on the latch. Light brown, amazing eyes met hers. "Show you?"

"Yes." Lysandra had no idea what she was thinking, but she ripped off her shirt and unsnapped her bra, letting it fall to the floor. As many nights as they had slept side by side, he'd never seen her naked since the first day she arrived. Now she stood there, her chest bare and her breasts bobbing with each breath she took.

Dante sighed, his anger deflating as his eyes caressed her over and over again. "That's not fair."

"Neither is you leaving."

He fell back against the door as Lysandra unzipped her jeans and shimmied them off her hips.

"Why are you doing this?" His voice came as a tight whisper.

"I'll do anything to keep you near me." She ran her fingers through her hair to undo the braid.

"To keep me near or to have a vision? What are your motives here, my love?"

Lysa crossed her hands over her chest, feeling the sting of his rejection. Every inch of her body heated with embarrassment. "I can't believe you even have to ask."

"I love you, Lysandra. I'll do anything to protect you. Anything." He dropped his eyes and turned back to the door, speaking over his shoulder. "Even if it kills me to do it."

He left without another word. Lysandra stood alone, feeling more foolish than she ever had before. She sank to the floor and buried her head in her hands. Sobs shook her body until she feared she would crumble apart. A piece of her heart had just walked out the door and the hardest part was, she couldn't be angry at him for it.

# CHAPTER TEN

## RYSE

RYSE STOOD IN THE LOBBY OF THE PALACE WITH HAMMON. RIGHT on time, Keona entered from one direction and Yankee from another. Ryse raised a brow in question.

"You and Hammon will go question her. I'll babysit the taxi. We can't risk letting the witch see her."

"Your concern is touching, but no thanks," Keona snapped. "I don't need a meter maid."

Ryse wanted to groan at their squabbling. Talk about oil and water. These two were going to drive him nuts. Yankee plagued him enough on his own. Keona seemed to ramp it up.

"What's the walking stick for?" Keona nodded her head at Hammon's carved wooden staff.

"It's a magic wand. Can we talk strategy?"

Ryse glared at Yankee. "Your mouth is testing my patience. I don't have time for this."

Yankee nodded and had the respect to look at the floor. He was usually mouthy and at times it was comical. Tonight, however, tensions ran high—especially with Hammon—and there was no room for distractions or delineations from the plan.

"Keona, what do you need to get us to a location?"

"I lived in London for a long time. Where do you want to go?"

"If you can get me to the shipping yard near Corringham."

Keona closed her eyes, and her head bobbled back and forth for a second. Then she opened her eyes and rolled her shoulders like a boxer getting ready to enter the ring. "Okay. I know a place."

"Hammon and I will go in. You two will stay close but out of sight. If she sees you, the whole Rogue community will know about you in seconds, I guarantee it."

"What will you do in there?" Keona asked, her eyes wide and her aura tinged with fear.

"We shall talk to the witch."

"And if she's not a good conversationalist?"

Hammon's eyes sparked with an inner fire. "Then we will quit talking and get the information we need the hard way."

"Well, that sounds like a party. Okay, everyone grab on."

"Guns?" Yankee said before he touched her arm.

Ryse nodded.

Yankee walked over to a seemingly innocent family portrait and pulled it open to reveal an arsenal of guns and ammo.

Keona walked right over like she owned the place and loaded up. "Perfect."

"You know how to use one of those, Taxi?"

"Piss me off and you'll find out, Meter Maid." She grabbed one of the black baseball caps in the stack and slapped it on her head. Not that she needed it; her hair was black as coal and her skin was brown.

The girl had spunk, and Ryse respected that. She strapped two guns on her thighs like it was second nature, stuck another one in the small of her back and covered it with her black shirt. Keona dropped three extra magazines full of cartridges in the pockets of her cargo pants.

"You going to war?" Ryse asked, slightly amused.

"Hey, not all of us have magical swords that appear out of thin air."

Ryse didn't know what to expect when Keona transported them out, but it wasn't nearly as bad as having his souls separated from his body like when he went to the Heavens. Teleportation was nothing compared to that.

Yankee stumbled but quickly regained his footing.

They were in the middle of an industrial park. They had left the Haven at 10:15pm, Tennessee time, making it four in the morning in London. They had little darkness left to work with. The sounds of the dock came from the east. Gantry cranes, unloading the freight that arrived during the night, clanked and thudded. The air breaks from the trucks let off a *psh* with each release. Keona had dropped them in the perfect spot. On one side was the docks, the other was the storage yards. If the docks were to the east, the witch's warehouse was to the north.

"This way." They crept through the line of trees and foliage that divided the active shipyards from the older, abandoned storage areas. They dodged in between containers that had sat so long weeds had grown around them. One open container had a squatter's bedding in it.

Ryse came to a halt when they had to cross a gravel road. It showed no signs of recent activity, but that didn't mean anything. The witch had her way of warding off people.

"There." Hammon pointed to a long warehouse. His eyes glowed with the use of his gifts. "She is there, with many others."

"What kind of signatures are you getting?"

Hammon's lips pinched together and his jaw tensed. "Those who are barely alive."

"I don't think we should go in there." Keona's voice was monotone and her eyes held a blank stare.

Hammon mumbled under his breath and waved his staff in her direction. Keona blinked and noticed everyone staring.

"What?"

"The witch has wards up. We must be careful." Hammon's eyes went white and he spoke in a language even Ryse didn't understand. He held out his staff and it rippled with power. "Stay behind me."

Slowly, the four of them approached the building. From the outside, it seemed harmless to human eyes. It was merely an old metal building with busted windows and birds as tenants.

Ryse, however, could see the truth of it. There were thick windows, blacked out. The doors had locks and security cameras.

"How do we get past the cameras?" he asked Hammon, who knew more about this witch and her abilities than anyone.

"Stay in the shadows." He held up his staff horizontally and it created a sheet of rippling air. "This will block her magic from us."

"What the hell is that thing?" Keona whispered.

"No time to explain." Ryse ducked behind Hammon and the others followed close as they crept to the doors of the warehouse. "Yankee." He nodded to the lock.

Yankee grabbed the thick metal and ripped it off the door with no effort at all. Keona gasped and her wide eyes stared at him.

Ryse pried open the door, flinching when it creaked.

Hammon led the way through dark halls, his staff covering their presence. The halls opened up into an open area, and the scene made Ryse's blood boil.

Olympians, dozens of men and women, were lined up in holding units, their bodies were pinned to metal plates. Metal shackles circled their necks, chests, wrists, and ankles. Machines were hooked to their veins and heads. None of them looked alive, but the monitors all showed faint heartbeats on the screens. Two of the bodies he recognized as Thracian soldiers who had gone missing in the field months ago.

In the back right corner was an enclosed area. Hammon headed for that room. Ryse signaled for Yankee and Keona to stay back.

It didn't matter if the witch felt their auras; Ryse was about to unleash hell on this wicked bitch. He kicked in the door of the room and there she stood beside a sink, washing blood off her hands.

"What the bloody devil are you doing here?" Her pearlescent honey-colored eyes darted between the two men. Her chocolate-colored skin took on a green undertone. "Hammon?" She scrambled to raise her hands and cast a spell, but Hammon was faster. The magic in his staff deflected her spells and he pinned her against the wall.

"There is no point fighting, Hellain. The gods have given me all advantage over you and I will not spare your life once more." Hammon shoved the staff right up against her throat.

"I should've killed you when I killed your wife, you bastard." Her eyes swirled and glowed. "How dare you come to this place?"

Ryse held out his hand and called upon the power of Ares. His long sword materialized in his hands. "You will tell me all about your experiments, Hellain, or I shall send you back to Hades once more."

She shook out her wild afro of curly black hair. "You can't. I'm under protection."

"I can and I will." Ryse rested the point of his sword on Hammon's staff, the tip piercing her throat. She struggled, but the magic of the gods held her still.

A single line of red blood ran over the tip of his sword.

"I will tell you nothing," she screamed, even as she fought to free herself.

"Wrong answer," Ryse whispered. He sent out his aura, a wave of anger blasting her against the wall. The concrete block cracked and she moaned. Her nose bled, but Ryse held no pity for her.

"It doesn't matter what you do, Master Thracian. You can't stop what they are doing. It's already in motion."

"What's in motion?"

Ryse pressed the blade further into her skin and she coughed. When she didn't answer, he said, "I saw Hades. I stood before him and heard the screams of his demons all the way from the depths. He took Salina Avondale after I beheaded her. There was nothing left."

Hellain's chest worked hard to keep air in her lungs and he could feel her fear; a heavy, lingering stench in the air. "How long did you stay in the flames the first time, Hellain? Wasn't it a century? You didn't learn your lesson the first time. Who freed you, Hellain?"

"What does it matter? You can't touch him."

"There are a thousand ways to torture you before you die," Hammon snarled, his black eyes glowing white. He whispered one of his chants, the kind that Ryse didn't want to know anything about, and Hellain screamed.

"Ashton!" she yelled and Hammon eased off. "Ashton Avondale freed me. He made a deal with a demon."

"What deal?"

"Fuck you."

Hammon's eyes glowed again, his whispers causing her body to spasm and quake. She cried out, screaming and writhing in pain.

"To bring the demons to earth again," she sobbed. "He wants to bring the demons back through Olympian bodies."

"Has it worked? Is that what the Prophet is? A test run?"

"Yes. Please, please stop!" Her body was plastered against the concrete wall, her head turned as far away from Hammon as possible.

"How many more are there?" Ryse continued his questioning. He felt no sympathy for her. None. This bitch was torturing Olympians to bring demons to his realm. There was nothing he wouldn't do to her if it meant getting the answers he needed.

"Only one success. The rest have failed." The veins in her neck popped out and her eyes clenched shut. Her face turned red and sweat dripped off her hairline.

"Is that what the bodies are for outside?"

"Yes." She screamed harder, her limbs thrashing about. "The women work best; they last longer." She coughed and blood seeped from her ear.

"How many, Hellain? How many women have you tortured?"

Her pearlescent eyes turned to his. Evil, pure and simple, shone from their depths. "Hundreds. He likes to eat them."

Hammon ceased his whispers.

"He was a mistake, Ryse. The boy volunteered. He was strong, so strong. But in the end, the demon blood was too much. He changed into something…unexpected. He was a shapeshifter. His Olympian blood and the demon blood created a beast." She coughed.

"Where is the girl? The one he captured yesterday?"

"I can't tell—" Her eyes bulged out of her head. "Ahh! She's coming. She's coming here."

"For what? Your experiments?"

"I don't know. He said to get a cell and infusion plates ready for two Thracians."

"Is the Prophet coming back here? Where is he?"

Hellain coughed up blood; her eyes drooped closed. "He'll be back," she whispered. "If he eats the flesh of a Grace, he consumes her power." Her head sagged and Ryse sent a burst of power through her body to wake her up. She wheezed and shook as if electricity had pelted her.

"I'm not done with you. What do you mean 'consumes her power'?"

Hellain struggled to breathe. "He gains more life." Her hand flickered to a notebook sitting on her table. "He's desperate. Why do you think he wanted your little Texan so badly? He's fading and regular Olympian flesh isn't enough. He needs more."

Red clouded his vision. Not only had this monster tried to kill Avery, but he was surviving on the death of Olympians. This would not stand. Blind, raging anger burned in his blood and the anger of the gods only fueled the fire. Ryse stepped over and grabbed the book from the table, scanning her notes and entries. "What are you doing with the bodies out there?"

"They are vessels. They are holding dormant demons."

Ryse's head popped up. "Excuse me?"

"He has an army, Ryse. There are thousands of holding areas just like this one all over the world. All they are waiting for is—" She coughed up more blood.

"What? All they are waiting on is *what*?" Hammon yelled into her face.

"Avery's blood."

Ryse's hands shook as he flipped the pages of Hellain's notes. They had found the results of Avery's bloodwork. They knew she could absorb the gifts of others. Avery's blood, the ability to capture all Olympian magic in one vessel, was exactly what the demons needed to secure their magic into Olympian bodies.

There were notes on Hanna's ability to make words a reality, Nikki's abilities to conjure objects, Brenden's ability to change into multiple animals, Dante's gift of blocking or canceling powers, and of course, a couple pages dedicated to him.

If they got their hands on Avery, all they would need was blood from a handful of powerful Olympians and they would have the recipe to feed life into their host bodies.

Ryse cussed under his breath.

Hellain started to laugh. It was a low, slow rumble that grew into a maddening holler. "You've already lost."

Hatred boiled up in him so hot and furious it erupted. Hammon, reading Ryse's body language, jumped backwards as Ryse brought his sword up and sliced the witch right in half, his aura blasting her body pieces against the wall.

"She won't be coming back again." Hammon stood upright and wiped blood off his staff. Ryse's aura had acted like a shield, keeping the gruesome explosion away from them. "May she rot in the flames of Hades for all eternity."

# CHAPTER ELEVEN

## KEONA

HER HEART RACED IN HER CHEST, BUT KEONA KEPT HER SHIT together. The rows of bodies lined up on metal plates nauseated her. The bodies all glowed with a strange redness in the chest area and her over-analytical brain wanted to inspect it closer.

"Don't even think about it. We're on lookout." Her babysitter grabbed her arm.

She remembered how he ripped a steel lock apart like it was a bag of potato chips and didn't try to test his hold. He would win.

"There's no one else in here. I'll be right back."

"Keona." He whispered her name in reprimand, but she blinked out anyway, right into the middle of the bodies.

One man's chest wasn't as bright as the others and she slid up next to him. The red glow of his chest captured her attention. It mesmerized her, pulled her in until she was so close she could feel his warmth. She hesitated but then reached up and touched his skin.

It scorched her fingers.

"Help me," he croaked, scaring the hell out of her.

Keona jumped back and then met his bloodshot eyes. The heart monitor picked up the spike in his pulse as he stared at her.

"Help…me." Moisture pooled in his eyes. His forehead crinkled as his dry lips trembled.

Keona couldn't catch her breath, completely freaked out that he wasn't dead. If he was still alive, were they all? Not knowing what else to do, Keona blinked back to Yankee.

"They're alive. They're not dead."

"I know they're not dead, but you will be if you ever disobey me again." He shoved her back behind his crouching position behind the wall. "Are you insane? Stupid, maybe? We are dealing with demons. You don't walk up and shake their fucking hands, okay?" He blew out a breath. "You could've been hurt…and then we would've been stuck here," he added to cover the concern in his voice.

Screams came from the room where Hammon and Ryse had disappeared.

"What are they doing to her?"

"You don't want to know."

"I think you're right." Keona crouched lower as the screaming increased. A shiver of fear washed over her from head to toe. Moments later, the room erupted and Ryse's aura knocked her and Yankee on their asses.

"Shit, come on." He jumped up and ran into the room with her hot on his heels. The both came to a skidding halt as they surveyed the destruction.

The back wall of the room was caked in human remains and splattered with blood.

"What the hell happened?"

"Oh my god!" Keona covered her mouth with the back of her hand and looked away.

Ryse exited the blood-spattered room and walked towards the lines of bodies.

"Kill them all," he commanded.

"What? Why?" Keona ran ahead and put her hands up to stop him. "They're still alive."

"They're not alive. They're hosting demons within them." He shoved the notebook at her chest and in turn shoved her out of his way.

The image of that woman was burned in her brain forever.

It was only trumped when Ryse went down the rows of Olympians and severed their heads. Keona glanced at the book he had shoved in her hands and she flipped through pages of pictures and journal entries of the experiments they'd done. Thousands. There had to be thousands of people who they'd played with like a high school chemistry set. Thousands of lives sacrificed, and for what?

The last entry read: *The subjects are surrogates for demons, whose spirits have already begun to ascend to their bodies. Each one has been injected with the minimum amount of demon blood and it is growing daily within them. Their souls are no longer their own. They will soon rise as the Prophet did, part demon, part god.*

Keona swallowed the bile rising in her throat. All these people, all these innocent Olympians were harboring demons, growing them like children under their flesh. There was nothing else to do.

Keona walked up to the man who had cried for help and lifted her gun to his head.

"Do it," he pleaded. "Please." He closed his eyes and took a deep breath.

"I'm sorry." Keona pulled the trigger, closing her eyes as the gun went off. The machine flat lined.

# CHAPTER TWELVE

## BRENDEN

HE PULLED OUT EVERY TRICK HE KNEW. BRENDEN USED HIS Olympian gifts, his human investigatory training, Thracian means of investigation—you name it. He had teams from Mexico to Canada sifting through traffic photos, flight records, car rentals, and shipping accounts. Hopefully, they would find the van spotted pulling into the park not long before it drove down the street leading to Evander's compound. Once it left the city, the cameras lost it. He'd contacted border patrol, the police in five states around Chicago, and his contact at the FBI.

In the last hours of his day, he'd sniffed every corpse, mentally catalogued the scents of all the dead Rogues, and arranged transportation for the bodies of Rogues and Thracians, patients, and clinic staff to be delivered to their families for burial.

All the families of the Rogues were under investigation by the local Thracians and Olympian leaders who looked to Evander as their authority. The man was well loved and sure to be missed.

Hammon worked his magic so that the human authorities knew Dr. Paul Smith had been in a horrible accident. They would never know what really happened in that mansion.

At midnight, he finally reached a place where he felt he could leave and everything was handled. Dinner at the palace had been a nice reprieve, but he asked Keona to bring him right back to the crime scene…scenes.

His last stop was the park and he went over it with a fine-tooth comb. Satisfaction ran through his veins as he picked up his cell phone to call Ryse.

"Confirmation. Ashton was here. When you and Hammon leave the witch, he needs to come check out the Olympian signature. He definitely used his powers here."

"That's what I needed. Will follow up." Ryse cut off the call without so much as a goodbye.

Brenden turned to see Nikki jogging up to him, her red hair swishing behind her. She was in active wear and running shoes. It might be late at night, but they wanted to blend in in the event anyone saw them.

"Call Ryse?"

"I did. My guys have taken over and Hammon will double check my findings here. I think it's time for some rest."

"Do we know when Keona will be done with Ryse?"

He shook his head as a yawn escaped his lips. "I say we get a hotel room. Avery is safe at home. We can go back tomorrow. Who knows when Ryse will be finished with that horrible woman?"

Nikki's mouth went tight, but she nodded.

"Could you, um, give us a lift?" He grinned at her and her scowl turned into a smile.

"Of course I can. Anyone looking?" They both glanced around, and he sniffed the air for passersby.

"All clear, Nikki the Magnificent. Do your magic."

Nikki closed her eyes and held up her hands, her fingers doing a dance in the air as the parts and pieces of a sedan appeared on the nearby street. No matter how many times he had seen her do it, watching a car appear out of thin air tripped him out every time.

"You're incredible, you know that?"

She shrugged it off as she opened the passenger door. "Kiss up all you want. You still have to drive."

He groaned and caught the keys she conjured and tossed his way. "Fine, but I'm picking the hotel, so get your Benjamins ready."

Nikki giggled at him and spread out her hands over her lap, spreading hundred-dollar bills out like playing cards. "Let's get a room with a jetted tub."

"Done." He reached over and touched her cheek, his heart completely and totally sold out to her, whether she knew it or not.

After securing a swanky hotel room for the night, Brenden immediately started a hot bath complete with a foot of bubbles resting on the water. He ordered champagne and chocolate cake from room service. They were happy to receive a very nice tip.

"What's this?" Nikki stared blankly at the bath with the champagne bottle on the ledge. Her whiskey-colored eyes were so full of innocence, even with everything she'd been through.

"This is for you." He sat the cake beside the bottle and poured a glass.

"For me?" She crossed her arms, that new defiant streak coming out. "You know I could've conjured all this."

"I know. But you don't have to. You've been a big help today, babe. You should relax." His canine senses picked up on the acceleration of her pulse; her aura flared with both excitement and anxiety. "I'll leave. Don't worry."

To his great joy, she caught his arm as he passed by. Those sexy bedroom eyes met his. "You've worked hard too."

Brenden took a chance and dipped his head, happy as hell when she lifted her lips to his. The rising heat in the bathroom had nothing to do with the hot water. She stepped into his arms and ran her hands up his chest to the buttons of his shirt, her fingers making quick work of them.

Of all the things he wanted in life, Nikki had to be number one. Since the first time he had seen her in the palace, she held his attentions. Her flaming red hair and hazel eyes, the way her waist flared into her hips, the curves of her ass, her perfect breasts that pressed against him now. Physical attraction had never been an issue, at least for him.

Once he caught the scent of her arousal when he was near, Nikki became his prey. She wanted him and he had known it for a long time.

He whispered her name as he wrapped his hands around the curves of the ass that had driven him nuts for months.

Their lips mingled and their tongues explored each other. Heat tingled all over his body from the top of his head to the bottom of his feet. Her lips made him feel like a live wire and sent blood soaring to his cock.

"Get naked," he commanded as he lifted her shirt over her head and peeled off the sports bra.

"You're so deman—oh god," she gasped as his mouth covered her breast. She ran her hand though his hair, pressing his mouth tighter against her.

Brenden couldn't wait any longer. His fingernails morphed into the talons of the bird inside of him. He hooked her thin pants in his talon and ripped them right down her crotch.

"Oh my." She giggled. "Get naked. Got it."

The sweet scent of her arousal hit his nose and made him growl. He fell to his knees in front of her and dipped his head to the source. "Damn, that's good shit."

Nikki stopped giggling and started moaning.

*Music to my ears.*

"Bren. Oh god. My legs are shaking. Oh god."

He lapped like the dog he was, eating up every sweet morsel

until her knees gave out and she screamed his name. If they weren't in a public hotel, he would've roared right along with her.

Then he scooped her up and sat her on the counter. The mirrors behind her gave him a perfect view of her bottom. He unceremoniously ripped off his pants and boxers.

Nikki's eyes were glued to his cock and it made every ounce of testosterone in his body salute. He'd never felt so powerful, so proud to be a fucking man than when he stepped into the V of her legs and she ran her hands over his chest.

He cupped her cheeks and stared deep into her hazel eyes. "Nikki, babe. Make sure you want this. There's no stopping once we start."

"Do you love me?"

He leaned his forehead to hers. "More than you will ever know. Do you love me?"

"It's the only thing I'm certain of."

Her words broke his heart and made him even more resolved to claim her as his own.

"Your bath will have to wait." Brenden wrapped her legs around his waist and took her to the bed. She deserved to be romanced and courted, but life didn't afford them that luxury. He would give her the best of what he had to give, here and now.

Bren examined her on the sheets, so beautiful. She was a true red-head in every sense of the word and she sent fire blooming in his gut. He wanted to worship her body, make her feel like royalty in his eyes. With as much gentleness as he could, he kissed his way up her legs, into the junction of her thighs. He pressed his mouth to her core, but kept going upwards over the dip of her stomach and the rise of her breasts. That sweet little body shuddered under his lips.

Brenden settled between her legs, spreading her wide to accommodate his big frame. He nudged at her entrance, pushing slowly inside her until he felt the resistance. There was no other way but to push hard and get it over with.

Nikki bit her bottom lip and whimpered as he broke through her innocence. Her mouth fell open and blew out a few breaths.

"I'm sorry, babe. I know it hurts."

A tear trickled down her cheek and she shook her head. "Give me a second."

Nikki had given herself to him, given him the one thing she could never take back. Bren nuzzled her neck and stayed connected to her, giving her time to adjust. Her arms wrapped around him and her fingers dug into his skin.

"I love you." He kissed her neck. "I love you." He nibbled her ear and kissed her over and over again. "I love you."

"I love you, Bren," she whispered, her voice trembling with her body.

Nikki's body tightened and she rocked her hips. His vision blurred. He rose so he could see her lovely face. "There's no stopping now."

"I'm yours."

Brenden braced his arm by her head and gripped her hip as he set their slow pace. His senses tuned in to her. All he could smell was her sweet arousal. Her pants and moans were music to his ears. Seeing her face flush and her body writhe under him sent satisfaction flowing through his veins. This was his woman and he alone did this to her. She was so close to the brink and he met her eyes as she cascaded over the edge. Her hand slapped the bed and gripped the blankets as if they could anchor her to the earth as he pushed harder and faster. The sensation of her body gripping his swamped him with pleasures he couldn't imagine until that moment.

Nikki's hands raked his back, pulling him closer. Her legs wrapped around his lips and took the building pressure as he thrust faster. When she finally hit her climax, her back bowed off the bed and she screamed his name.

That was all it took to make him lose control, knowing she was right there, flying with him. He collapsed on her chest, his head against her pounding heart.

"I had no idea sex was so wonderful," she giggled.

"And that was your first time. Imagine how much better it will be next time."

"It gets better?" Her voice cracked with surprise.

Brenden braced himself above her. "Oh yeah."

Nikki smiled and put a hand over her thundering pulse. "I don't know if my heart can take it."

"You can. You will." Brenden bent to suckle her breast and he fondled the other. "I can't wait to explore with you. Positions. Angles. Foreplay." He kissed his way back up her neck to her sensitive earlobe. She shivered when he did that.

"Oh, my."

Brenden carried her to the bath and sat behind her. He leaned back in the tub and closed his eyes as Nikki lavished him with love and affection and kisses, so many perfect kisses.

When the water chilled, Brenden carried her to the bed and loved her thoroughly until she passed out in his arms, her red hair like flames in the rising sunlight.

He sent Avery a text that he and Nikki were resting and he would let her know when they needed transport. It bought him a few hours at least. For those hours, he wanted to hold the woman he loved and pretend like they were just a couple of normal people and that the world wasn't falling apart around them.

# CHAPTER THIRTEEN

## KEONA

"THIS IS BULLSHIT," KEONA SCREAMED AND SLAMMED HER FISTS down on the table the next morning. "My sister is out there, god only knows what's happening to her, she could be hurt, and you're not letting me go search because I don't have *your* stamp of approval? I'm sorry, what are you the god of again? Arrogance?"

Yankee stood and leaned over the conference table, meeting her eye to eye. "I'm an Elite, that's who I am. You think just because you can vanish that you're a badass? You're going to get yourself killed and you're no good to your sister dead. You ignored a direct order last night."

"Ugh!" Keona grabbed her scalp. "They were vegetables; they weren't going to hurt me. Nothing happened." She turned to Hayden; surely he was her ally in this. "Tell him, Hayden. Tell him we need to leave today, right now. This is coming up on twenty-four hours after the kidnapping. It's crucial we find her fast. Your mate is out there and we have to find her before the Rogues kill her or worse."

Hayden took a deep breath and gave her what could only be called a patronizing smile. "No one wants to find her more than you and I do, Keona. But Yankee is right—"

"Boom." Yankee's smug grin almost pushed her over the edge.

"—you're not prepared, not to fight demons and Rogues. Hell, the Elites can hardly fight demons."

"I am trained. My mother was a fierce warrior and she taught me everything she knew." Keona fisted her hands at her side. "You might not have understood why she betrayed the race, but you can surely remember her reputation. My family is from Athenian blood. Our females are fighters."

"That doesn't mean shit." Yankee rolled his eyes.

"Listen, asshole." Keona swung around, ready to put this mouthy punk in his place.

Hayden stood to place a hand on her shoulder. "Keona, don't bother with him. Yankee, for the love of the gods, watch your mouth."

The crass Thracian shrugged. "What do you want me to watch it do?"

Ryse held up his hand and everyone in the room closed their mouth. "Keona, you are in the home of the Thracian Training Center. If there is one thing we know how to do here, it's train fighters. You are a fierce fighter, but you're not a soldier. You have to prove that you're capable of following orders."

"We don't have time," Keona argued. Why didn't they understand this? Her sister was kidnapped and they wanted to have a freaking conference about it?

A single brow raised on Ryse's forehead and his powerful aura slapped at her until she dropped her eyes.

"You're correct. We have no time for this bickering. I will not send troops into the field unprepared. We don't know where your sister is. We don't know if she is even on this continent. We now know of the warehouse, which is under surveillance along with the entire coast of Southern England. If you say you have a telepathic bond, but she's unreachable, then that leaves two possibilities. There's some sort of mental block or she's dead."

"She's not dead." Keona and Hayden spoke the words in unison.

"I believe you." Ryse stood and pulled at his black cotton shirt. "We have every asset available to us working on finding her. But I will not permit you to run off into danger unnecessarily. Value your own life, please."

Avery once again was the voice of reason and compassion. "Brenden's still out there. You took Hammon to him this mornin'. Together, they're like a bloodhound on crack. Their talents workin' together are much more sensible than you runnin' off half-cocked. I know this is hard, but stop for a moment and think about the best course of action."

Keona sat down and tried to contain her emotions. Fear and anger warred with each other and, so help her Zeus, if Yankee didn't wipe the smug look off his face, she was going to carve it off with one of her knives.

"In the next forty-eight hours, the women will have intensive training. Men, take the women to the obstacle course first. Let's get them nice and warmed up. After we see where you are physically, Lysandra, I want you to go with Hanna and Hayden. He needs to go back into a sleeping state and we need to know if he receives anything from Piper."

"Yes, Master." Lysandra nodded, her eyes meeting Dante's for a brief moment and then shying away. The big guy clenched his jaws and turned his head to Ryse.

*I missed something there.* The two of them were unusually distant this morning. Normally, their eyes held such affection for one another, it was puke-worthy.

"Cutter is going to work the bodies with Ixion and his hounds.

That leaves Dante, Yankee, and Philippe to focus on the offensive and defensive training. Keona," he slid a cell phone down the table, "you're on call."

"Got it." She picked up the phone, a brand she was familiar with, and slid it into the pocket of her pants. She knew exactly what her gifts and talents were; she didn't need to be told. When and if Brenden and Hammon found something, she was to go. If Ryse found something, she was to go. If Piper contacted her telepathically, she was to go.

It was what she did.

"Philippe will work with Avery. See if she has any of the other elements besides fire at her disposal. Yankee, you work with Keona. Let's see if you two can learn from each other instead of just bickering. I'll make the rounds for all of you. First, we start with the obstacle course."

Keona wanted to groan, but she kept her reaction to herself. Ryse didn't seem open to discussion today…or ever.

She glanced over to where Yankee sat with his hands clasped behind his head, his chair leaned back on two legs. He kissed at her and smoke rose from her ears. She blinked to his side of the room underneath the table, kicked out the back legs of his chair, and blinked right back to her seat before his back hit the floor. Avery covered her chuckle, but it was so fast, no one else even looked her way. Yankee cussed as the guys teased him for being clumsy.

He rose to his feet and glared at Keona. She winked and puckered her lips.

Avery grabbed her by the arm and pulled her from the room before Yankee could even the score.

The group drove together around a picturesque lake to the Thracian Training Center. The towering red brick buildings appeared as if they'd just been built, even though they were many centuries old. Keona was amazed and slightly frightened at the hundreds of Thracian soldiers who lived in the dormitories. If you overlooked their ridiculous size and pounds of packed-on muscle, the campus could be mistaken for any college in the world.

"They aren't nearly as relaxed as the first time I came up here." Avery peered out the window with a sigh. "None of them are playin' football or sittin' in the grass studyin'." She glanced over to Ryse. "It seems colder."

He put his hand on her neck. "We are at war, my love. It's time for them to be the soldiers Ares created them to be." He addressed the ladies in the van. "All of the trainees' general studies have been suspended. Math, history, theology—all of it has ceased. Right now, the men prepare for warfare and battle. They are working on their specific gifts, nothing else."

"Do your students not need the Elites as their teachers?" Dynasty, who was right in the mix of things, *holy shit*, was a strikingly elegant woman. Her long fountain of silver and gold hair reached her bottom even when it was braided, like now. Lavender eyes, like nothing Keona had ever seen, held an abundance of knowledge.

"They have excellent teachers, Mother." Ryse smiled at her, the only other person besides his mate who ever received such affections, from what Keona could tell. "The Elites oversee all the curriculum for the students and take turns visiting each class to stay abreast of their progress. Right now, you need the Elites more than the Thracian students. Their teachers are potential Elites and the cream of the crop."

The van stopped beside an obstacle course. "What fresh slice of hell is this?" Keona swallowed hard.

"This is our beginner course."

Avery made a shrieking sound in her throat. "If this is the beginner course, I'll never be a darn thing more. And I've worked with the god of fire, seriously."

Keona chuckled. Avery's southern accent was both adorable and irritating, if those two adjectives could ever mingle. When the native Texan came out in her language, Keona cringed. She'd been all over the world and heard a myriad of languages and accents. Texan was something that could be trashy or endearing. Luckily, Avery leaned more towards endearing most of the time.

Ryse pointed to a small building to the left. "In there are locker rooms. Each of you has a locker filled with workout clothing, thanks to Nikki."

Avery reached over and patted the redhead on the back. *Ah, right. Nikki.* She was the Shadow Lady who was publicly punished for playing an unwilling part in killing the Grand Deity. She was still trying to learn names, but she knew all about Nikki.

"Go change and be back here in five."

Keona hadn't dressed out with a bunch of random women since she was in junior high school. Even then, she'd taken her clothes to the toilet stalls and had some sort of privacy.

Not today. The ladies stripped down, including the widowed Queen.

"You realize you don't have to do this, right?" Avery whispered to Dynasty as she pulled on her green cargo pants.

Dynasty buttoned her long-sleeved green shirt. A golden sword was embroidered on the breast. The lavender-eyed woman smoothed down the shirt that was much too mundane for the likes of her. She shook her head and lifted her chin with pride. "Of course I do. I will not sit on my throne any longer. It is time for people to see that Deities are more than pretty faces with crowns on their head. We were born with powers just like Thracians. Somewhere out there is a girl I shall soon call my daughter." Dynasty met Keona's eyes. "If Piper is a Divine Grace and the gods have destined her for my son, you and your sister are my family." The Queen draped her arm around Avery's waist. "I nearly lost this daughter, I will not lose Piper too. Not if I can help it."

Keona nodded once and turned away before she anyone could see her tear up. No one here even knew Piper and yet they were ready to go to war for her. A queen, who could just as easily order an entire regiment of soldiers to fight battles in her name, stepped down from her throne, donned the bland attire of army fatigues, and prepared herself for physical training with her troops.

*Now that's a leader I can get behind.*

When all the ladies were dressed and standing before Ryse and his Elites, Keona's stomach turned into a volcano of nerves and acid. What if these trained killers, these men who were Marines, SEALs, and demigods rolled into one, laughed her off and sent her packing?

Master Ryse examined them, clasped his hands behind his back, and took a deep breath. "Let's start with some basics."

The Elites led them through a series of push-ups, sit-ups, running laps, and drills. Keona was nowhere near winded, but others had trouble.

"You know," Avery bent over with her hands on her knees, panting, "bein' dead for two months is a real downer for your muscle tone. I'm just puttin' that out there."

"You were dead for two months?" Keona took a swig of water.

"Yep, had a real nut-kicker out-of-body experience. Body was here, soul was in Olympia. My body basically sat on its ass for two months." Avery shrugged like it was no big deal, just another day in the life of an Olympian.

Keona closed her eyes and shook her head, unable to imagine such a thing. "Wow. So when I saw Zeus bring you back from Olympia, he was basically reuniting your body and soul?"

"Pretty much. I don't recommend it. Hurts like a sumbitch." Avery winked at her.

Yankee clapped his hands slowly, a mock applause to their previous workout. "Okay, girls. Now that you've completed the kid stuff, it's time to move on to the course."

Keona's fist itched to punch the smugness right out of him.

"Since our Thracians train here and then integrate into the human military populace, every basic training facility for every branch of military in the world mimics what we do here. By the time our Thracians complete their training, they can get into any high-ranking military position in the human world." Yankee pursed his lips and looked Keona up and down. "For you ladies, we just want you to finish the basic combat confidence obstacle course without crying over breaking a nail."

"Samuel?" Dynasty lifted a brow at him and pursed her lips. Her tone was motherly; stern but affectionate. It was akin to being called by your middle name as a child.

Yankee stifled a grin and bowed his head. "My apologies, my Queen. With all due respect, you're in my house now."

Dynasty stepped up in front of the others. "Then train us and watch your mouth, son."

This time, he openly grinned and waved his arm elaborately towards the field. "Milady," he said with a deep bow.

Dynasty patted his cheek as she led the group over to the wooden wall that stood at least eight feet high.

Dante awaited them. He had eyes like Dynasty, eyes that could never be seen by the humans. Dante's eyes were the color of sand; pretty, but *other*.

"The first obstacle is the low wall. Your objective is to scale the wall and get to the other side. This will promote upper and lower body strength. I'll demonstrate. Thracians train with a fifteen-foot wall. We've shortened this one."

He jogged up the wall, jumped up, and caught his arms on the top, then swung one leg over and pulled his body over the other side.

That looked easy enough.

Dante emerged from behind the wall. "Who wants to try first?"

Keona's hand flew up into the air. "Me."

# CHAPTER FOURTEEN

## HAYDEN

H E FLICKERED IN AND OUT OF DEEP SLEEP. THERE WERE LUCID moments when Hayden could feel the effects of Hanna's command floating in and out. She spoke one word to him. "Sleep."

He drifted off without pause. His body was completely relaxed, safe in his bed. His mind wafted between dreaming and full consciousness.

*It's dreadfully frightening to be trapped in your own body.*

As much as he tried, he couldn't force himself to find Piper; partially because of his own anxiety. He felt like a child forced to take a nap. When he needed to sleep, wanted to sleep, he couldn't.

Instead of focusing on how much he needed to sleep, he tried to focus on why. He imagined Piper—thank the gods he finally knew her name—wearing that long white gown, her silky black hair falling about her shoulders. Dark eyes, full of life and mischievousness and most of all, kindness, were ringed in long thick lashes. Her lips beckoned him, full and always smiling.

Beautiful.

*"Hayden?"* The voice was a whisper.

He sat up in bed and put his feet down in the grass.

*Grass?*

Hayden stood up on a thick carpet of green grass. His bed sat in the middle of the gardens.

"Piper? Are you there?"

*"I'm here."*

He searched and searched but didn't see her. "Where are you?"

*"They're taking me away. I have to be careful."*

Hayden sat on his bed and closed his eyes. This was a dream. The gardens didn't matter; all that mattered was her voice.

"Yes, be careful. Keep your aura tight. Do you know where you are?"

*"I'm in a van. The best Cain and I can tell, we are headed north. We've crossed the border."*

Thank the gods Cain was with her. He sighed in relief that she wasn't alone.

"Have they mentioned anything that would lead me to you?"

*"They mentioned the Prophet. I'm so scared, Hayden."*

"It's okay. Me too. Keona is here with me. She's in the Haven. We are all looking for you."

*"No!"* Her voice was urgent and strained. *"It's her they want. She's a teleporter. Keep her safe. It's Ashton. Ashton Avondale. He took me from the park. If he gets Keona—"*

"Even Ryse can't stop your sister, my precious angel." Hayden found himself crying and laughing. "She is a force of nature."

*"Evander? Did Evander make it?"*

Hayden's heart shriveled in his chest. "No."

*"Oh no. Oh gods, please no. They were meant to be together."*

"So are we, and I'm going to make sure that at least one of you has a happy ending. Think, my angel. What can you tell me that will help? What do you smell? What do you hear?"

*"Stay with me, Hayden. Please stay with me."*

"I will, I promise."

Piper never answered, but there was a sense of her presence still there, like background noise. Everything within him focused on that noise. It was tires going down the road, an engine shifting gears, muffled whispers from a man close by. If Cain was with her, he could only assume it was him. Through all the noise, Piper was forcing herself to stay asleep. It must've taken all of her effort.

Hayden could almost feel her thirst, her hunger, her need to use the bathroom and breathe fresh air. There were three bodies, but only two heartbeats, two people he could hear breathing.

He concentrated so intensely that for a split second, he thought he was in the van with her.

Then she was gone. The white noise ceased and the voice in his head left.

"Piper? *Piper?*"

# CHAPTER FIFTEEN

## ASHTON

ASHTON RECOGNIZED THE GIRL AS SOON AS HE SAW HER. THE LONG midnight hair, obsidian eyes, a face that could start wars… the face of her fucking mother. He'd never forget Marlaina Nadal. She'd nearly exposed him and ruined his connection with the demons. That stunt she pulled twenty years ago cost him a valuable asset. Teleporters were rare and many of them kept their powers hidden.

As they should.

Ashton was lucky to have snagged that bald monk of a teleporter when he did. He had to kill the man's entire family before he would submit. But it was worth it to have the luxury of instant transportation.

And now he would again.

Twenty years after Marlaina Nadal sacrificed her life to save her daughters, Ashton peered down into the eyes of a woman who would give him the advantage over the Castilles.

The girl tried to cover herself as best as possible as she stood before him. The twenty-four-hour van ride from Chicago to Nova Scotia had not been kind. Then again, neither had his men as they'd transported the girl, one living Thracian, and one dead one.

Ashton kicked back in his velvet chair and crossed his legs. "It's okay. We'll get you cleaned up shortly. You do smell horrid." Someone had lost control of their bowels during the trip, but he didn't think it was her. "Listen closely, lamb. It is very important to find your sister. I'm sure you understand how valuable she is."

"I won't help you. I know who you are and I'll die first."

Ashton's lips twitched. He liked her spunk. Her mother had the same spunk. This child would crumble just like Marlaina did. "Little lamb, there are much worse things to fear than death. I don't need to kill you. That seems so…final."

"What have you done with the others from the van?" She shook with every word.

"You must be thirsty," he said, sipping his own drink, ignoring her concern for the others. "Are you hungry? I doubt those two brutes fed you, did they?"

She shook her head.

"Don't worry about them. I shot them as soon as they delivered you. You know how it is, loose ends and all."

Her gasp was music to his ears. She should be frightened. Making people hurt was his specialty and he enjoyed every cry for help.

There was something about her, though, something he couldn't put his finger on. He didn't just want to hurt her; he wanted to shag her first, maybe at the same time.

"I'll make you a deal." He leaned over, his elbows on his knees. "Why don't you go get cleaned up and we'll have dinner and talk about what's going to happen next?"

"What do you want from me?" Her bottom lip trembled and it was the saddest, most pathetic thing he'd ever seen.

"You'll find out soon enough, little lamb." He winked at her and waved his hand, dismissing her from his sight. "Take your time and clean her up. Dress her like a lady. I'll not have a rat dining with me. If she gives you any problems, kill her."

The maid scuttled the girl out of the room. Ashton turned to Xavier. "Where is the Thracian?"

The older man stood right behind him, right where he should be. "In the basement."

Knowing that one of them had lived gave him great satisfaction. Thracians made the best test subjects. "Who's with him?"

"Maxim."

"Good." Maxim was a masterful artist of torture. He would find out exactly what the Thracian was made of. "Are we on schedule for the shipment?"

"Yes."

"Did my parents make it home?"

"Yes. General Gastone called me to confirm that you were returning home soon."

"And you told him…what?" Ashton glanced up at Xavier.

"That we were traveling and you were quite heartbroken over Salina's death. You're unable to come right away but will be home shortly."

"Good." He sipped his whiskey. All the pieces of his plan were falling right into place. "Any word from Hellain?"

"Not for a few hours, sir. Not a surprise, really. She's not the most stable of characters."

He rolled his eyes. "True. She's probably naked in the woods somewhere doing some kind of hocus-pocus ritual." The witch was useful, but for shit's sake, she was out of her bloody mind.

"We did secure the book from Evander's estate. The scientists are going over it now."

"Anything else of value?"

"Computers, security cameras, things like that."

"How many men did we lose?"

Xavier cleared his throat. "All of those who went into the house and clinic."

Ashton turned in his chair. "Are you fucking kidding me?"

"Evander had twice as many Thracians there as what we were told, for a total of seventeen. They all died but the one, but all eighty of our men perished at their hands."

"Let me get this straight, one Thracian died in the park with the girl, so *sixteen* Thracians took out *eighty* men who had the element of surprise on their side?"

Xavier met Ashton's eyes. "Thracians are superior to Olympians in their combat skills. It's how we were created. You want a powerful army? Quit taking riffraff Olympians and putting guns in their hands. The eighty men were poorly trained and barely used their powers to save their own lives."

The fact that Xavier didn't hesitate to challenge him burned him up inside. Ashton stood and pulled at the collar of his shirt, removing his tie. "How long have you been with me, Xavier?"

"Your whole life, sir."

Ashton rolled up his sleeves. "Then what in Hades' name makes you think you can speak to me like that?" He punched the General in the gut, using his gift of physical manipulation to enhance the power of the blow.

Xavier doubled over, his face red and straining.

"Tell me again how Thracians are superior?" He brought his elbow down on the back of Xavier's neck and sent the mighty Thracian to the ground. "If my troops are poorly trained, it's your fault, General." He sneered the last word and walked away. "Get on your feet."

"Yes, sire. Sorry, sire."

"Remember, Xavier, you rise or fall with me. Make fucking sure we rise. Now, if you will excuse me, I have a dinner date."

# CHAPTER SIXTEEN

## PIPER

NEITHER OF THE MAIDS GAVE THE VIBE OF BEING A KILLER, BUT one never knew with Olympians. Piper didn't put up a fight. The two women, neither of whom made eye contact, undressed her, bathed her, shaved her, washed her long hair, and made her brush her teeth. They combed out all the terrible knots and then fixed her hair, applied her makeup, and helped slide a slinky, sexy blue dress over her bruised and tired body. Her fairly large breasts were on display and spilled over.

"You're fatter than last girl," the older woman huffed in a heavy Russian accent.

Piper blanched and whispered, "What happened to the last girl?"

The cold gray eyes of the woman sent chills up her arms. "She fight back." The woman shrugged as Piper covered her mouth with her hand. "She not nice girl." The woman's eyes softened and her shoulders slumped slightly. "Please, do not give me reason to kill you, pretty girl."

Piper shook her head rapidly and lowered her gaze. She did *exactly* what the Russian lady asked.

*Oh gods, Keona. Where are you?*

It took all her self-control not to gorge on the decadent food. The table was set for a feast, even though only Piper and Ashton sat together. Servants came and went, filling her glass, cutting her meat, wiping up a speck of potato that had fallen from her fork to the table linen. They all would stare at her until she met their eyes. Then their gaze would dart away and they would skitter back to the kitchen for something.

"You look divine in that dress," Ashton said, raising his glass of red wine to his lips. The dark glint in his eyes frightened her more than anything. Now, instead of brushing her off, his expression was one of a predator. He ate his meat slowly, enjoying every morsel, chewing every bite as if he could prolong the flavor.

The older Russian lady, who stood in the corner of the room, cleared her throat.

"Thank you." Piper spared the woman a glance, but didn't address Ashton. She pushed around the food on her plate, taking small bites of the meat. The taste and texture was familiar, but she couldn't think what it was. Her mind had more important things to focus on. Moments passed in silence. Ashton watched every move she made and she kept her eyes down, her enemy in her periphery. Each of his bites was slow and deliberate.

Finally, she set down her fork and leaned back in the high-backed chair. "I want to see the others," she whispered.

"Not right now. You need to eat."

"The rich food makes me ill."

"If you're ill, you will be seen to by a Paean. Since I don't know the extent of your sister's teleportation gift, I think I'll keep you close by." He wiped his mouth and threw his white napkin on the table carelessly. "Your mother was an amazing asset. You can't imagine how ironic it is, having a Nadal woman back under my roof."

Piper's heart beat faster at the mention of her mother. Keona was in greater danger than ever. She knew all too well what lengths Ashton would go to in order to procure a teleporter. There was no body count too high.

"Hand of the gods, so they called her. A teleporter with such skill she could move entire cities if she wanted. She worked for all the royal families many years ago, was richly rewarded for her services until one day, she snapped. She went rogue, killed her husband and her children, and went to work against the Deities."

"That's not how I remember it." Piper's knees shook under the table, but she kept her aura locked up tight, only revealing what would seem a natural amount of fear. Thank the gods, Ashton couldn't see the terror that turned her veins to stone and choked her of oxygen.

He leaned over the table, his eyes searching her for something. "Do tell, little lamb. How do you remember it? You were just a child."

Piper took a drink of water, her throat dry and scratchy. It also gave her a moment to consider the best way to tell the story. "She was hunted by the Rogues. My father was murdered, my sister and I were taken hostage." Piper's mouth trembled at the memories. "You forced her to do things, horrible things. She sacrificed herself so that my sister and I could be free of you."

One side of Ashton's lips curled up. "My, that almost makes her sound heroic." He took another bite.

"She was." Piper sniffled and wiped a tear from her face.

"Your mother was weak. She threw away her life. You and your sister were well taken care of. You had everything you needed."

Piper shook her head. "Except our father and our freedom."

"Don't cry, little lamb. Things will be different this time around."

"I won't help you."

"Calm yourself. You don't have to do anything." He finished his drink and snapped his fingers for a refill. "You just have to exist."

"I want to see the others." She rubbed her bare arms.

Ashton flicked his hand at her. "You will finish eating."

Against her will, Piper picked up her fork and stuck a piece of meat in her mouth. She ate until her plate was clean, even things she didn't like.

When she was finished, her stomach hurt, she was so full. All she wanted to do was throw her food right back up.

"I want to see the others." She swallowed back the overflow trying to come up.

Ashton narrowed his eyes at her and took a sip of whatever was in his glass. "Are you sure about that? One was dead. You really want to see him?"

"I want to see the others."

Ashton nodded and shrugged. "So be it." He stood and Piper mirrored his actions—not on her own. Ashton had complete control of her body and it scared her to death.

She took his arm when he extended it and they walked together through the extravagant mansion full of gold leaf and marble, shining crystals and antiques. The last mansion she'd been in was Evander's home. It had been luxurious, well loved, and cozy, as far as big homes went. This place, however, was ostentatious. It was over the top, a monument built to money, a shrine to the owner's ego. The suite she was locked in was another example. The furniture was huge and no doubt worthy of a hefty price tag. The frescos on the walls were fresh, though they were made to look aged. Even the toilet was gold. The shower had ten different sprays, a cavern wrapped in marble and gold.

"Do you like it?" Ashton petted the wall of marble. "It's from the quarry of Calacatta della Gharardesca in Italy. The finest stone, worked with a little Olympian magic to fit my needs."

"Your needs seem to be met sufficiently." He made her absolutely sick.

"They are." He smiled wide. "Having a Deity father has its advantages. This is only one of my ten estates across the world."

"Why are you so eager to destroy your source of riches?"

Ashton took her long black hair in his hand and lifted it to his nose, inhaling her smell. Piper jerked free. He chuckled.

"I'm not eager to destroy my father. I love my parents, despite their ignorance. I'm eager to show them the truth. My father needs to see the gods for what they are."

"They created us. Haven't you figured out they could end you easily?"

Ashton lifted his hand to encompass their surroundings. "Where are they? Hades protects me. He is the only god worth bowing to."

"They were there when your sister lost her head."

Ashton rounded and grabbed her by the neck. Lifting her off the ground, he squeezed tighter and tighter until her vision went blurry and she was gasping for air. Her legs dangled and her pulse ran in overtime.

"Watch your mouth, little lamb, or I will slaughter you like the pathetic animal you are." Ashton dropped her and she fell to the floor grasping at her neck and sucking in as much air as she could to refill her lungs. She dropped her forehead to the cold marble. It took all of her strength not to cry, so much so that her head ached from the effort.

Ashton picked her up by one arm and towed her down a hall-way and down a staircase to a door manned with a guard. The soldier, wearing red fatigues, like the Rogues who invaded Evander's house, unlocked the door and opened it for them.

The smell hit her first. Human feces and blood, something rotten and decaying. All the rich food stuffing her stomach tried to come up once again. Piper covered her mouth. She stopped before Ashton stepped over the threshold of the door.

"Nope." He pulled her in. "You wanted to see the others and so you shall."

He tugged her by the arm to the first room and Piper instantly regretted asking to see *both* of the men who were in the van with her.

"No!" she screamed. "No!"

"This is your albino friend or at least what's left of him."

Nicholas' corpse lay in multiple pieces on tables. Piper couldn't contain it any longer. She turned her head directly to Ashton and let all the contents of her stomach spew on his leg.

"Oh, for fuck sake." He threw her down on the cement floor. "You asked for this, you fucking bitch," he screamed over her. "I gave you what you wanted."

"You're a monster," Piper yelled back at him, tears falling in sheets down her face.

"You want to see a monster?" Ashton's eyes went black and Piper crawled backwards away from him. Ashton grabbed her by her hair and dragged her down the hall to a row of cells.

Piper yelped and screamed, the pain like nothing she'd ever felt before. Strands of her hair ripped out until she wished it would all let loose.

Ashton threw her in front of a cell. "There's your monster."

In front of her, behind the bars of its cell, was a real monster; a creature from her worst nightmares. The red-scaled lizard leapt from the shadows towards the bars and she shrieked. Now that it was in the light, she saw the black talons, the humanoid eyes, and the recognition within them.

When the beast touched the bars of his cell, they rippled yellow and sparks flew. The beast howled out.

"Calm down." Ashton flicked his hand at it. "There's no need in hurting yourself, friend. She's not your dinner."

"That'sss a ssshame," it hissed. "Ssshe looksss juicccy."

*The Prophet.*

This was the creature that had been taking Olympian women all over the world.

"I'm hungry. You promisssed."

"And I shall deliver." Ashton pointed to the room where Nicholas' body had been. "It's Thracian on the menu tonight."

Piper gasped, her body shaking uncontrollably. They were going to feed Nicholas to this monster? "N-n-no."

Ashton knelt down in front of her. "What was that, little lamb? You want to take his place?"

She shook her head fast and backed away. "No. No. Please, no."

"Then I suggest you not deprive our friend of his meal." Ashton stood and held out a hand.

She was too frightened not to take it.

"We have one more person to visit, and this one you'll want to see."

Each step she took was a challenge. Her knees wobbled and knocked. Dearest Zeus, she didn't want to see what was in the shadows of the next room.

"My good friend Maxim has been asking your pal a few questions. It seems he's reluctant to answer." Ashton took her chin between his fingers and looked right into her eyes. "I want you to persuade him to talk."

Ashton opened the door to a pitch-black room and flipped on the lights. Bright white filled the room, so glaring she had to close her eyes until they adjusted.

"Piper?" A weak but familiar voice whispered her name.

Cain hung ten feet in front of her, his body completely naked and bleeding from multiple cuts. Angry bruises covered his blood-crusted skin. His eyes were swollen from the beatings and drops of red were dried to his face like macabre tears.

"Cain!" Piper shoved off Ashton and ran to him. She lifted shaking hands to his battered face. "I'm sorry. I'm so sorry." She sobbed and petted him gently.

"Don't do it," he huffed. Each word took monumental effort. "You can't."

Her hands were tied. If she healed Cain, her aura would be open and her powers revealed. If she didn't, he would surely die.

Piper turned to Ashton. "Why?"

"I don't think you comprehend how much I need a teleporter." He stood behind her and rubbed his hands over her shoulders, brushing her hair away.

Cain jerked against his chains, but he didn't have the strength to do much more.

"I need your sister," Ashton whispered in her ear, wrapping his arms around her waist and pulling her back against him. "If you don't help me, I will have no choice but to allow Maxim to continue questioning your Thracian friend here." His hands splayed over her stomach and one ventured towards her groin. Piper tried to pry his hands off, but he was in control. "Make up your mind, little lamb. Does your friend here get to rest or not? His blood is on your hands."

"No," Cain groaned. "Say nothing."

Ashton flicked his fingers and Cain wailed, his voice hoarse and dry.

What did she do? Two lives rested in her hands. If Ashton got his hands on Keona, he would make her a weapon just like he did their mother. Did she risk her sister's life in order to save Cain? He suffered needlessly for her, had sacrificed himself for her sake.

"I know this is hard for you. How about a compromise?"

His mock sympathy only fueled her anger.

"Why don't we give Cain a break for tonight? You can rest and think about the smartest decision for you and yours, then we will talk about it again in the morning?"

Nothing that came from his lips could be trusted, but maybe she could buy some time. Keona or Hayden would find her; she only needed time.

Piper nodded her head.

Ashton's hand cupped her breast and Cain jerked again in his chains, growling at him. "Don't worry, Thracian. I'll take good care of her tonight." His tongue trailed up the side of her neck to her ear and Piper fought him, turning her head and prying at his hands.

Compared to his powers, she was helpless and he knew it. He laughed as he dragged her out of the room and flipped off the lights.

"Cain!"

"Now, now. Don't fight me, lamb. It only makes it more fun for me."

No matter what she did, someone would die. It might as well be her. Piper screamed as loud as she could and kicked Ashton's knees, causing him to stumble and fall.

He cussed and spit at her. "Bitch." Pain blossomed in her cheek as he struck her. Her skin burned from the strike.

Ashton raised his hand and gained control of her body. Tears ran down her cheeks as he forced his lips on hers and his tongue invaded her mouth. She desperately wanted to bite him or hurt him somehow. But he was in control of her physically.

"Keep fighting," he said, gripping her hair with force. He shoved one shoulder of her dress down and fondled her breast. "It turns me on even more."

Piper had to think. Ashton might have control of her body, but her brain was still hers. What would Keona do? "I have no problem killing myself to save my sister. Cain would do the same. Take what you want, bastard. I'll never betray her. Besides," she huffed out a breath with the same attitude Keona would use, "only a pathetic ruler has to force women to his bed. You want me? Take me. And while you're on top of me, I'll be reveling in the fact you're so inadequate—"

Ashton silenced her with his hand and laughed, actually laughed at her. For a moment, she thought her fiery tongue had backfired. "Stupid girl, I don't have to beg. I don't have to force anyone." He snapped his fingers and the maid fetched three women who appeared far too happy to be there. All three of them looked plucked from a fashion magazine. "Who are you compared to them?"

Piper fell to the floor in a heap.

"Lucky for you, I don't like to fuck rats. Guards! Take her to her room and lock her in. If she tries to escape, kill her."

The men scooped her up. She was dead weight. None of her muscles worked, like the connection between her brain and her body had been severed.

His eyes danced with the knowledge of his victory. Piper was taken up the stairs. The last thing she heard was Cain's voice screaming out her name.

# CHAPTER SEVENTEEN

## PIPER

"YOU MUST RISE UP NOW." THE RUSSIAN WOMAN SHOOK PIPER awake. "He asks for you."

She had forced her body into a deep sleep in anticipation of what might come with the morning. Her nightmares were of dead bodies being devoured by demons.

"What will he do with me?" Piper asked, already on the verge of hysterical tears.

The woman didn't answer, only held up Piper's jeans and hoodie. "You dress."

Desperation made Piper fall at the woman's feet. She pleaded, "Please, what will he do to me?"

"This is up to you." She dropped the clothes on the floor and left the room. "Hurry," she said just before she closed the door. The sun wasn't up yet and the room was illuminated with only one lamp.

Piper had been left in the dark last night and she'd been happy to be that way. This morning, she wanted to know where she was.

The view out the window was spectacular. Had she not been the captive of a murderous lunatic, it would've been picturesque. They were either on an island or a peninsula. At the edge of the rocky property was the sea. It stretched for miles in front of her and she feared that was her destination. There were smaller islands around, nothing inhabited, but they were lush and green this time of year. The panes of the glass were cold; they had definitely traveled farther north than Chicago.

Piper searched the room, trying to find anything that would have a name, a label, a logo on a pen, anything that would give her a location. The luxurious furniture had nothing. The drawers were all empty in the bedroom and bathroom. There was nothing but blankets in the closet.

"Time to go," the woman said as she entered the room once more. Behind her were two guards. "Do not fight, pretty girl."

Piper trembled as they escorted her right out of the mansion and down to the docks. The air was bitter and crisp in her lungs.

"Good morning, little lamb." Ashton waited at the end. He was bundled up, along with his men. Behind him was a yacht carrying a single freight container. "I hope you slept well. You've had plenty of time to ponder your situation here, so let's put all our cards on the table. I'm taking you, the Prophet, and your Thracian back to London. Now," he waved a hand towards the vessel, "your Thracian and the science experiment are together in the crate. You, my lovely," he pushed her hair off her face, "have a choice to make. You can take a warm car to the airport and travel on my luxurious private jet, a trip that will only take a few hours. Or you can ride in this container, which is headed to a ship with thousands of tons of freight on the open ocean for eighteen days with your Thracian. Keep in mind, if you're cold now, crossing the ocean in only that hoodie is going to be chilly. I can't remember if we put food in there for the Thracian or not?" He rubbed his chin and frowned.

"He'll die." Piper's teeth chattered and her body shook with the cold.

Ashton grimaced in thought. "Maybe. Maybe not." His snicker was thick with bloated power. It left an oily, sickening taste in her mouth. "If he dies, my creature will have more food. If he lives, my creature will have more food. So you see, either way," he held out his hands, balancing his options, "I'm not too concerned. You, on the other hand, have a choice to make. We can contact your sister from the car, the plane, my stunning home in London. You can live the life of luxury. If you behave, there will be no need for all that unpleasantness of last night."

She didn't believe anything he said, except for when he said he didn't care about Cain's outcome. She, on the other hand, had to make sure he lived. "I'll never help you and I'll never hand over my sister."

Piper jerked free of her captors and walked herself right down the pier to the container.

"Eighteen days at sea will either change your mind or kill you. Either way." He held up his hands again and laughed as he walked back up to the house.

"Move it." One of the men in a red uniform pointed a gun at her back and pushed her into the shipping container.

At the back, in another cage, was the Prophet. He hissed and snarled, laughing when he saw her. "A feassst, delivered to me."

Piper didn't focus on him, because Cain was chained to the right wall. "Cain!" She dove for him, but the guards caught her and threw her against the left wall to bind her in her own chains. "No! No!"

He didn't move, not even to breathe, but she could feel his aura.

The men locked her wrists in chains and closed the doors of the crate, locking her in cold darkness. The boat motor revved to life and they bobbled back and forth as they moved across the water.

"Cain? Cain? Can you answer me?"

"I'm here." He moaned and groaned, his chains rattling with his movements.

Piper couldn't see anything except for what lay in the rays of light shining into a few holes on the container. "What have they done to you?"

"Worry not for me. Are you harmed?"

"No," she lied, not wanting him to know that her scalp still ached from where Ashton had dragged her by her hair. "I'm fine."

"Thank the gods."

"I'm scared, Cain."

"You ssshould be, sssweet meat." The Prophet scraped his talons on the bars of his cage. "Thessse barsss won't hold me the whole trip." The metal screeched as he wrapped his claws around it and twisted.

Her heart nearly exploded in her chest. What had she done?

*Oh dear Zeus, please help me live through this.*

# CHAPTER EIGHTEEN

## ASHTON

ASHTON'S CHOPPER HOVERED OVER THE BAY, AND HE WATCHED with his own eyes as his container was lowered onto the cargo freighter. The red box was one of three thousand Lego pieces stacked on that ship. His just happened to be right on the outside so he could make sure he saw it leave the bay, and he would see it arrive in London.

He didn't head to the airport until he saw the ship pull anchor and head into open waters.

"The plane is waiting, sire," Xavier reminded him through the headphones.

Ashton nodded and the chopper swirled around to head back inland.

*Foolish girl.* He wished she had chosen differently. The back of the jet held a comfortable bed and he would've liked to get her in it—forced or not, he didn't care. She was beautiful, though foolish.

Out the window of his plane, the world grew smaller and the ocean took over the land.

"You know he will eat them both after eighteen days." Xavier leaned his head over. "You didn't put the wards on his cage. It's only a matter of time before he breaks out."

Ashton smiled his most charming smile at the stewardess who brought him a glass of whiskey. "That's the plan."

The busty blonde bent over to hand him the drink, purposely giving him a view down her shirt. "My Prince."

"Thank you." He winked at her.

"If there's *anything* I can do for you, all you have to do is ask."

"How very kind, beautiful lady. Very kind indeed." Ashton glanced over at Xavier, who was licking his lips as he examined her backside. "You know, my friend here is a world renowned warrior. Perhaps you could show him some of your *kindness*. I happen to know he loves blondes."

She turned around and held out her hand to Xavier. "Come, warrior, I have something to show you in the back."

Xavier, being the good little bitch that he was, looked to Ashton, who nodded and saluted with his glass. The two of them disappeared into the bedroom and only moments later, he could hear the giggles and moans. He would be well taken care of.

There was no better way to seal a man's loyalty than to give him what he desired and remind him who supplied it. For Xavier, it was women and power, and the ability to break the rules beaten into him by the gods and the Thracian teachers who had trained him all those years ago. He had married because he wanted a woman, he'd grown as a Thracian because he wanted power. Two things Ashton had in abundance. Now that Xavier's desire for other women was out in the open, he could use the information.

"You're all alone, my Prince." Another busty woman in uniform came towards him. Her dark hair flowed around her shoulders. This was why he hired them, to keep him occupied on long journeys. "I think you need some company." She unbuttoned her shirt and Ashton observed the scene, growing harder with each button she loosened. Yes, he had more women than he knew what to do with.

"I think I need you on your knees."

As her head bobbed up and down between his legs, Ashton sipped his whiskey and thought about the Nadal girl. He'd left her with no food, one jug of water, a half dead Thracian, and a flesh eating monster that was bound to figure out how to escape his cage. He still had no teleporter, but at least the teleporter would suffer, thinking she could have saved her sister. There was a sense of victory in that.

Odd, he almost hoped she lived.

# CHAPTER NINETEEN

## AVERY

I T TAKES APPROXIMATELY TWO HOURS FOR A BODY TO BURN WITH Olympian accelerant: a mixture of Avery's fire gift and her impatience. Two hours was too long to stand in a room full of people mourning the person whose pyre they surrounded. Two hours of wishing you'd done more, wishing you'd known, wishing that death would take a holiday, for Pete's sake.

Avery stared at the blazing body of Evander Castille, Ryse's cousin. Her mate stood beside her, unmoving, as if he were the dead one. Ryse's eyes never flickered away from the fire. She knew, because she kept glancing up at him every five seconds. His jaw was as sharp as a razor's edge and his nostrils flared. Ryse didn't cry; he didn't hardly blink. His boots were planted firmly in the temple's concrete. Like all the other men in the room, his right hand was fisted over his heart, the left behind his back.

Such strength.

Such bottled-up emotions.

Avery took a deep breath and tried not to fidget. This was his cousin and she had to pay her respects in the way of his people. Truthfully, the whole scene made her crazy. Considering her primary gift was fire, that was saying something. The temple was packed with people who might've known Evander, but the majority stared at her, the spotlighted circus freak. She wanted to turn around and scream, "Yeah, folks, I came back from the dead. Now quit your gawkin' before I set your asses on fire too."

Finally, *thankfully*, Ryse stepped forward and about-faced to address the congregation. "Our family will mourn for three days, as is tradition. We ask that all of you also pray and meditate for the family and friends of Evander." Ryse showed his first sign of emotion as his face pinched together and he cast his eyes to the floor. "He shall truly be missed." Without another word, he marched out of the temple and stopped only to nod at Keona. She bowed her head to Ryse but didn't move. Neither of them had spoken about what happened in London the night before.

Avery kept her mouth shut until she and Ryse were behind closed doors. "Baby?" She lifted her hand to touch his back and hesitated. He was known for not accepting touch, for shying away from something as mundane as a handshake. Since the very first time they'd met, Ryse had touched her. His mate was the exception to every rule. At least, she hoped.

In the last couple months, Ryse witnessed his father's murder, visited the land of the gods, executed a woman he had known since childhood, whipped Avery's best friend for murder, and dealt with countless other issues along the way. Not to mention the whole situation with her: find her, mate her, watch her get stabbed, watch her burn, watch her come back from the dead, guard her body while her soul was in Olympia, and then finally get to see her back in one piece.

The man was due some peace, but that wasn't about to happen.

"Do it." His deep voice brought her back to the moment. He

peeked over his shoulder at her. "Touch me, please." The last word wavered, so thick with emotion, it broke her heart.

Avery raised her hand and traced a line down his spine. The trail was tattooed under his shirt.

Ryse sucked in a shaky breath and let it out in a rush.

Unable to wait another heartbeat, Avery wrapped her arms around him from behind and leaned her head in that perfect dip between his shoulders. It was made for her. *He* was made for her.

As soon as she closed her arms around him, his massive body relaxed. It broke her heart to hear him sniff and clear his throat. Ryse might be a demi-god, he might be known as a heartless executioner and punisher to their people, but with her, he was different. The façade broke and he let everything show. Negative energy radiated from him, his aura whirled around her like a twister. With every shuddering sob, the torrent built. Avery clenched her eyes closed and held on for dear life as the pictures on the wall swung from the nails, the blankets blew off the bed, and the lights flickered.

Ryse held up his fists and roared, sending his aura out in a mushroom cloud. The desperate agony in his scream ripped Avery's heart into pieces. It shattered along with the crystals in the chandeliers and the light bulbs of the lamps. The walls creaked and moaned under the pressure.

Avery's arms tightened. She wasn't letting him go, not now, not at a moment like this. Everyone within the castle walls would've felt the blast of his aura and known his pain. The aftershocks still shook her and turned her legs to jelly so she could barely stand up.

The wind quieted, the pressure in the room dissipated, and Ryse took a deep breath.

Avery clung to him still, afraid to let go, even though it seemed the storm had passed. "It's okay, baby. I got you."

Ryse huffed and sniffed again. "Yeah? Stand on your own two feet." His torso shook with another heavy, unsteady breath.

Avery stood and righted herself as he turned. "I meant

emotionally. Don't ever count on me physically. Your ass is too big for all that." She wiped away her own tears and tried to smile.

Ryse cupped her cheeks and stared into her eyes. His lashes glittered with wetness. "How did I ever survive without you?"

Avery leaned into his palms and closed her eyes. "All you did was survive, darlin'. I promise you, one day when this war is over, we'll live, truly *live*. You'll be happy again, baby. I know you will."

He wrapped her in his massive arms and hugged her close. "I can't wait for that day."

Avery soaked in his aura and inhaled his scent. Even in what he thought was a moment of weakness, he was so strong in her eyes. Zeus and Rhea had delivered her a man who would forever sit on a pedestal in her mind. Wrapped in his arms, she felt safe, needed, wanted. Loved.

"Before every man in history became great, he was tested. This is just your test, Ryse." She looked far up into his deep brown eyes. Her Thracian warrior towered over her short frame. "I'm so sorry about Evander. I know you were tryin' to cultivate that relationship."

Ryse nodded and stepped back. "Evander and I were never close, mainly because I was never close to anyone, even as a child. He is, was, too much like Hayden; carefree, playful. We never had much in common, but he was always one of my favorite cousins. I appreciated certain things about him, you know?" Ryse leaned against the poster of the bed and crossed his arms, leaning his head back against the wood. "He had a strict work ethic, he had a heart for our people, he made millions working the stock market just so he could run his clinic as a non-profit." He shook his head, his features pinching together. "Of all the people in the world, why him? Why did he have to die?"

"According to Keona, he gave his life defending the people in the clinic. Evander fought as bravely as any Thracian. He'll be remembered as a hero."

"It didn't help, though, did it?" Ryse stood straight and his face hardened into the killer she knew all too well. "Those goddamned Rogues killed everyone, Avery. Unarmed men, women, and children. *Children.* I'm glad you didn't see what I saw last night. It's like they want to eradicate their own race. Damned Ashton Avondale." He fisted his hands, then stretched his fingers wide over and over again. Frustration radiated off of him and it was completely understandable. Avery was ready to hogtie and beat Ashton like a filthy rug… then she could set him on fire.

"Your mother is going to keep workin' on Dante's memory. Lysa won't say she saw Ashton in her vision, but she alludes to it. I think she's afraid of outright accusin' someone." Avery made the bed back up, anything to take her mind off the last few hours. "I told her that if he's innocent, he doesn't have a thing to worry about, now, does he?"

"I think Lysandra is too kindhearted to be the person pointing the finger. Being responsible for uncovering Ashton might make her think his blood will be on her hands. I will not place her in that position. She's trustworthy, no doubt in my mind. We have what we need against Ashton."

"And where did you find this smokin' gun?" Avery flopped down on the duvet and closed her eyes, pleased when Ryse's weight shifted the mattress beside her.

"The truth always surfaces. The witch told me what I needed to know. And when the time comes, I'll slice that bastard's head off just like I did his sister's."

They turned towards one another and propped their heads up on their hands.

"How are you doin' with that, by the way?" Avery ran her hand over his chest. She thought about how upset he'd been after beheading Salina Avondale. They'd grown up together, they'd had common ties.

Ryse's lips pinched together. "She's not the first person I've killed, Avery. She's not even the first woman."

"Perhaps." The next words made her swallow back bile. "But she was the first woman you ever slept with."

Ryse immediately turned away. "Why would you even bring that up?" He scrubbed his hands over his face. "Bloody hell, will I ever stop being haunted by that?"

"Ryse." She reached for him, but he rolled off the bed and went to the bank of curved windows that overlooked the gardens. *Me and my big mouth.* "I'm sorry, baby. I only mean that you had a connection with her. Good, bad, or ugly, it was there. You knew Salina, grew up with her, played with her as a child. Doesn't that affect you at all?"

A shiver danced on her skin when his cold eyes locked on to hers. "No. And if you want to become a warrior, you'd better learn to not let it affect you either." Ryse headed for the door. "Come on. Pity party's over. We've got work to do."

# CHAPTER TWENTY

## ASHTON

B Y THE TIME HE LANDED IN LONDON, ASHTON HAD SCREWED both the women on the plane and so had Xavier. He was happily sated and ready to go see the progress of his army. After a long phone call to his grieving mother so that she knew he was home but not able to face the palace without Salina in it—or some bullshit like that—his car drove him down to the ware house by the shipping yards where his cargo would arrive in a few days.

Xavier, Maxim, and Ashton were the only ones who knew of the location of Hellain's laboratory. It would stay that way. The amount of magic used to conceal it had nearly gotten him killed.

The car pulled up and Ashton immediately knew something was amiss. There were no wards. There were no auras coming from inside. Nothing.

"Shit." He feared the worst, and his fears came true. After Xavier cleared the area, Ashton stepped into a stinking, bloody mess of bodies. Anger boiled up inside him until he couldn't think straight.

"Maxim," he barked. "Get on a plane right now, go to our other facilities. I want status reports."

"Sire, we have people—"

"Go," Ashton bellowed, his voice echoing throughout the expansive building. "I want your eyes on it. Not fucking *reports.* I want your bloody eyes on every single one."

He didn't like it, but Maxim took off.

Xavier examined the slash mark going down the back wall of the tiny apartment Hellain had lived and died in. "If this was Ryse, he's found the teleporter."

"How did he know?" Ashton closed his eyes and pinched his temple. "How the fuck did he know about this place?"

"He knew of Hellain, sire. Hellain was the one who murdered Hammon's wife. In return, the gods gave him a staff that protects him from black magic."

Ashton whirled around to glare at his General. "And why wasn't I informed about his connection and this staff before now? That's important information." He yelled the last sentence, losing his calm.

"With all due respect, sire, you didn't inform me of any of this until recently. However, Maxim, who is ranked beneath me, knows where all the facilities are? How is that?"

"Oh, don't get your bloody feelings hurt. I had to make sure you weren't going to lie down and suck Ryse Castille's dick like your son has. You know now. We have five other facilities throughout the world. Each holds one hundred surrogates. It's our army, Xavier. We needed something stronger than Thracians to fight Thracians."

"What else are you not telling me? What do I need to prepare for?" He clasped his hands behind his back.

Ashton narrowed his eyes at the older man and took a deep

breath. "According to Hellain, we need Avery's blood to awaken the demons, but only after she's been blood bound with Ryse."

"Why?"

"Avery is capable of taking on the powers of the blood she receives. When she has her official ceremony with Ryse, she will not only have the powers she contains now, but his. With that blood, we can awaken our army."

"Says who?"

"Hellain." The twenty questions was getting aggravating, but he suffered through it. Xavier was a man of details. It was what made him a good soldier.

"Hellain, as in the woman whose brain matter is currently painting the wall in there?"

Ashton rose up in his face, satisfied to see Xavier shrink down a fraction. "I mean the woman who was cast into Hades and yet returned back to Earth. Yes. Her brains might be gone, but her tactics are not. Hellain and I have made quite a few discoveries together."

"What do we do about all this?" Xavier motioned to their slaughtered test subjects.

"We take what machinery we can and burn the rest to the ground. We need to secure the other facilities and make sure no one finds them. I don't know how much information they pulled out of Hellain before they killed her. We can't take any chances."

Xavier stepped close and leaned in. "He will know you're involved, Ashton, if he doesn't already."

"I'm beyond worrying about Master Ryse Castille. Once I've taken his woman and raised my army, there will be nothing he can do to stop me."

Xavier walked away to begin disassembling the hibernation units for transport. Ashton pulled out his phone and called his man who was aboard the ship.

"How is my cargo?"

"Cargo is secured and we are on schedule."

"Good." Ashton couldn't lose the Prophet; he was the link between demons and Olympians. As much as they needed Avery's blood, they needed his too. "Feed it the Thracian. Keep the girl alive."

With all the subjects of this location gone, he had to depend on the other labs. These incubators had to work. Ashton closed his eyes and saw Salina's head being severed from her neck. He remembered her final thought to him:

*You're next.*

# CHAPTER TWENTY-ONE

## BRENDEN

BRENDEN STOOD IN AN ABANDONED BUILDING NORTH OF CHICAGO. It took him and Hammon two days to find the place where the Rogues kept the boy. His scent was all over a mattress and blankets in the corner.

"There was very little magic used here," Hammon said. "It is surprising."

Brenden nodded, his animal senses picking up the same vibes. "It's like they don't want to be Olympians or something. When we fought them, they relied on their guns for protection, not their gifts. One or two fought with magic, that's it."

"They're not trained to use their gifts. Olympians have become so reliant on Thracians for their protection, they will not even use magic to save their own lives."

With a near silent pop, Keona showed up with Ryse, Avery, Dante's friend Ixion, and two hounds.

"That's a first." Keona popped her neck. "Never had to blink out dogs before."

"Is that what you call it? Blinking?" Ixion asked, a little *too* excited about it.

Keona grinned. "That's what my sister calls it."

"Cool." Ixion smiled brightly, annoyingly. The obvious thrill of adventure was written all over his face. "Okay, where do we start?"

"Here." Brenden pointed to the mattresses lined up on one of the walls. "From what I can scent, the same people who slept here were at the park. I'm betting these are our kidnappers."

Ixion turned the dogs loose. The white glow of the god's powers took over his eyes and he tilted his head to the side, almost like one of the hounds he was controlling. The tall length of his body went still and Brenden glanced over at Hammon, who shrugged.

Ixion spoke in a different tone when he channeled his powers. His voice was monotone and deeper, lacking the enthusiasm from before. "One scent was in both the house and the clinic, but not one of the bodies we searched. The scent of him was faint, possibly someone casing the place." The dogs went to the boy's bed. "He was here a long time. The scent is deep. Tears. Lots of tears. No blood. Traces of the mother. Not recent. Food and water. Medication of some sort."

"They were holding him hostage," Ryse said, taking in the scene.

"Drugging him, if I had to guess." Ixion's eyes lost the glow. "It's in the saliva on the pillow where he drooled."

Ryse's brows raised in a quick expression of surprise. "Interesting. You can tell all that from the minds of dogs?"

"Yes, Master Ryse. Dogs are highly intelligent creatures. Their sense of smell is—"

"Fascinating, I'm sure." Ryse held up a hand to stop his prattling, and Brenden covered his laughter with a cough. It would take the young Thracian time to get used to Ryse's no-nonsense manner.

"Okay, so we can conclude that the maid was the inside man because these assholes were holding her son."

The dogs howled and barked at something behind a temporary wall. All the men ran around to check it out.

"I believe they just found another crime scene." Ixion cleared his throat. "It's the boy."

The dogs sniffed at a pool of blood and drag marks that led to the garage door on the east side of the building.

Brenden studied the scene. Based on the blood splatter, the boy was low, maybe on his knees, execution style. He fell forward, left this pool of blood, then his killers dragged him to the van where he lay long enough for lividity to set in.

"How far are we from Evander's compound?" Ryse asked.

Brenden had driven it this morning. "An hour and a half." Plenty of time for the boy's blood to settle and the texture and ridges of the van's flooring to be imprinted on his skin. "These weren't professional killers. Look at the mess. They left a damned bloody boot print, belongings, clothing, tracks, and fingerprints everywhere."

"Brenden, do your thing. I want to know the make of the boots, the tread of the tires, all of it."

"These idiots are almost making this too easy." Brenden bent down and examined the boot print. "I need more guys on this crime scene."

"Got it." Keona saluted and blinked out.

"She really is handy-dandy, isn't she?" Brenden completely understood why teleporters were sought after. Instant travel was great.

Keona blinked back five men with their equipment and wide eyes. "Thanks for flying Keona-Air; you are now free to move about the crime scene."

"Good one." Ixion laughed, his voice echoing off the walls of the empty building. "I get it…because…you kind of fly, right?"

Everyone stared at him.

Redness painted his face and he quit chuckling. "Sorry."

Brenden went through his usual procedure of pictures, evidence tagging and gathering, and documentation.

"Hey, this looks important." Ixion had found a laptop and was typing away. "It's encrypted. Hold on…yeah, for the record, one-two-three-four is not a secure password."

Brenden peered over his shoulder. "You know how to hack computers?"

"It's not really hard when the people setting them up are idiots, but yes, I can hack into most anything."

"I thought you were a dog whisperer?" Keona sat on the bed beside him.

"As fun as it is to be in their minds, they sleep a lot. I had to figure out something else to do."

"Anything pertinent?" Ryse glanced over his shoulder.

"Right now, it looks like a lot of porn and video games." Ixion hunched over the screen. "Hey, I like that one."

"Yuck, dude." Brenden blanched.

"I agree, this game is really graphic; lots of blood and guts."

Keona chuckled and then busted out laughing. She waved her hands when Brenden met her black eyes. "Sorry. He's just so oblivious. It's cute."

Ixion's head tilted to the side. Finally, the light bulb illuminated. "Oh! You thought I meant the porn. Yeah, wow, took me a second." He chortled and shook his head. "That's not it. Oh gosh. I'm going to shut up now." He slapped a hand over his face, which was now bright beaming red.

Brenden couldn't help but feel for the poor guy. Ixion couldn't meet Keona's eyes for the rest of the day.

As much as he liked doing his job, Brenden's mind kept going back to Nikki. He kept visualizing her naked and panting underneath him. At one point, he stood by the window of the building and stared out at nothing at all. He sighed, wishing he could take her back to that ritzy hotel and make love to her all over again. She was so beautiful, so passionate, so uninhibited. He had no idea sex could be so incredible. To think, she was waiting for him at home.

"I know that grin." Ryse stood beside him.

"Sir?" Brenden straightened up and focused on where he was.

Ryse narrowed his eyes at him. "I take it things are going well with you and Nikki?"

"Yes. Yes, sir, they are."

"Does she still wish me dead?" One of his dark brows arched on his face. "Or you, for that matter?"

"I'm too lazy to hold a grudge." Brenden shrugged, but he avoided Ryse's eyes.

"You've done fine work with this case so far."

Now it was Brenden's turn to question him. "You feeling sentimental, old man?"

"Maybe." Ryse inhaled deeply and crossed his arms over his chest. Bren was no little man, bigger and bulkier than most humans, but Ryse made him feel small in comparison. "Maybe I'm just giving credit where it is due."

Brenden huffed.

The two men were silent for a moment before Ryse let out another deep breath. "I'm glad you two have each other."

"Me too."

"Got something really good here." Ixion waved his arm in the air.

Ryse whirled around. "Son, if you're talking about porn again, I'm going to bust your balls."

Ixion's eyes rounded and his mouth dropped. "N-n-no, no, sir."

"I'm joking," Ryse said, completely devoid of a smile or anything that resembled an expression of humor.

Brenden elbowed Ryse in the gut.

"Ha." Ixion faked a smile. "You're a funny one, Master Ryse." His eyes darted between Ryse and Brenden. He swallowed hard, trying to keep up like he wasn't freaked out.

"What you got, kid?" Bren slapped him on the back.

"Uh, right. These are maritime charts and shipping schedules. I found the website in the browser history. They weren't clicking on anything particular, but all the ships they did search for left from the same port up north. So I went back into the GPS and this place came up." He showed the guys the last location they searched on the map.

Ryse cursed under his breath. "I know where they are. Keona!"

She jumped to her feet. "Who do you need?"

"All of them."

"Got it." She blinked out.

A snarl crossed Ryse's lips as he glared at the screen. "We're going to Ashton's estate in Nova Scotia."

# CHAPTER TWENTY-TWO

## AVERY

THE HELPLESS LOOK IN DANTE'S EYES AS KEONA BLINKED HER AWAY nearly broke Avery's heart. Even Ixion and two of his dogs could be teleported. Dante had to be angry; he had every reason to be. Keona's method of moving all the Elites and soldiers wouldn't work on him. Dante was stuck, cemented to the palace as she ran off to face danger. What Thracian wouldn't be mad?

There was no time to discuss the issue. Keona dropped them right in the back yard of Ashton's estate in Nova Scotia.

"Damn it, Taxicab," Yankee whispered, crouching down instinctively. "Why don't you just ring the doorbell next time?"

"Shh," Ryse snapped. He touched Hammon's shoulder.

The tracker's eyes were already glowing, searching for the signatures and auras of other Olympians in the house. "All are low-level Olympians. No Thracians. Two females, upstairs. Four males, two downstairs in a basement, one outside patrolling the front, one at the back." He lifted his chin. "We're about to have company."

"Grab on." Keona blinked everyone into the living room on the main floor…everyone but Yankee.

"Oops," Keona said as Yankee glared at her through the window. He crouched behind a shrub and when the guard came by, he knocked him out with one punch. Yankee took the guy's radio and flipped Keona the bird, then hustled around the side of the house.

"Cutter," Ryse said, motioning towards Yankee with his chin. Cutter slipped out of the house in graceful silence.

"Avery, Ixion, secure the females upstairs. The rest of you, with me to the basement."

Avery, Ixion, and his two Dobermans crept up the stairs. Her hands were tensed and ready to produce fire at any moment. The dogs led the way, using their noses to locate the females in the massive mansion. When they had the first one located, Ixion held out a hand, halting Avery from entering.

The two dogs pushed through the door and began to growl. Avery didn't know what language it was, but she knew cussing when she heard it.

"Do you speak Russian?" Ixion whispered.

"I'm southern. I barely speak proper English." Avery shook her head and the woman in the room finally screamed. "Well, *she-it*."

Avery charged into the room, fireballs in her palms, and stood between the animals. "Silence."

The older woman fell to her knees, her hands clasped together, pleading in Russian. Tears fell down her face.

"Where's the girl?"

"She gone." The woman shook her head, her black and gray hair falling out of her bun. "She gone for days."

"Where?"

"With prince, she with prince. Please don't let it eat me."

Avery blanched. "Ew, why would the dogs eat you? That's gross." Avery turned her head to Ixion, who stood in the doorway, his eyes glowing as he controlled the dogs.

All she saw was a hand raised and a kitchen knife come down into Ixion's shoulder. He yelled and fell forward as Avery sent both her fireballs flying. They incinerated the other woman instantly.

Avery pulled the knife out of his shoulder blade and sent a fast, hot bolt of fire to cauterize the wound.

"I'm okay, I'm okay." Ixion kept his control of the dogs, even though sweat beaded on his forehead. "Better me than you."

"*Povyeska, povyeska.*" The woman pointed to the bathroom but didn't move from her place on the floor. The dogs had her pinned down. "Bandage."

Avery ran into the bathroom and searched the cabinets and drawers, finally locating a first aid kit. She had no knowledge of nursing, first aid, any of it. Hell, she was doing good to strap on a Flintstones Band Aid when she had a paper cut. Ixion needed more help than what she could provide. Pressure, she knew he needed pressure, so she held a bandage over the gash.

"Call off the dogs. We have to get you downstairs."

"What about her?"

Avery met the pleading eyes of the older woman. If she was an Olympian with crow's feet and grey hair, she was at least five centuries old, if not more. "She's coming with us."

The woman had trouble getting back up on her feet and it was all Avery could do not to go help her.

On second thought, it was pretty easy to resist because Ixion already had a knife wound and Avery wasn't too keen on going through all that stabbing and dying drama again. Once was enough.

"We stay behind the dogs. You just herd her right on down and we'll get the heck out of this rodeo together, m'kay?" She kept her hand pressing down on his cut, his blood still seeping out and over her fingers.

The dogs worked in sync to guide the all-too-willing hostage down the stairs and into a dining chair Avery put in the corner. She laid Ixion down in a recliner, facing the woman, and conjured up a nice loaded gun to put in his hands. "You stay here. If she moves, shoot her."

The woman's hands went to the seat of the chair as if she were holding on for dear life.

"Don't move. Do you understand?" Just for insurance, Avery pointed her finger at the floor and left a flaming semicircle cage between the woman and the dogs.

Avery dashed off to the staircase leading to the basement. She eased down the stairs, sticking close to the wall, fire ready to fly. Her heart thudded in her ears and she feared someone would hear it as loudly as she did. The basement was silent and a maze of corridors and rooms were carved out of the rock.

A hand came around her mouth. She ducked and spun, ready to fry whoever was there.

She cursed when she recognized him. Cutter.

He held up a finger and moved to get in front of her. He waved her forward, down the first hall. Now there was light and voices she recognized.

Inside the room lay one Rogue soldier, his dark red blood mixing with his red uniform and the apron that had seen many more massacres.

"What were they doing with the body?" Hammon asked, his eyes glowing. "There is no dark magic being performed here."

Intuition had the words spilling out of her mouth. "They ate them."

Everyone turned to stare at her like she had three heads.

"The woman upstairs begged us not to eat her. Why else would she say that?"

"Savages," Cutter muttered from beside her.

"I have something," Brenden called from down the hall. There was a row of cells and in the back of one of the cells was a pile of bones.

"They were feeding something." Brenden sniffed the pile. "These bones are fresh."

"Magic is strong here, blood magic. Evil. Out, Brenden, you do not need to be near it." Hammon waved him out of the cell.

"The Prophet," said Ryse. "They had the creature in here. He eats our kind. Hellain told us as much. She said he would return to her warehouse. I bet that's where he's headed now."

"She's with someone who smells of Keona." Ixion hobbled down the hall, his dogs sniffing and investigating each and every cell. "Yankee is with the woman. The dogs caught a scent and I had to come."

"You're hurt?" Keona went to his side and examined his wound.

"I'm fine. Will you kneel so the boys can smell your hair?"

"Uh, sure?" Keona glanced around for confirmation from the others, then bent over, letting her long black ponytail fall over her shoulder and into the face of the Dobermans.

They went back to sniffing the hall and Ixion's eyes glowed. "Her hair is on the floor, the girl who smells like you."

"Piper." Keona's eyes met Avery's. "She was here."

Now that the dogs and Brenden had a trail, they followed it all over the house. Avery stayed back with Ixion and Keona and the housekeeper inside as Brenden tracked Piper's trail right down the pier.

"She is on boat," the woman sniffed. "They put pretty girl who look like you on boat and go."

"Where? Where did they go?" Keona was frantic by this point. They had proof, undeniable, that Piper had been here recently.

"They take the monster too. She go with the monster." The woman's chin quivered and her eyes flooded with tears. "He will eat her like he eat the others."

"Avery?" Keona met her eyes again and it tore her up to see the desperation and fear there. She turned to Avery for affirmation that her sister would be okay, and that was exactly what Avery gave her.

"We'll find her, I promise."

*Please, please, Zeus, let us find her in one piece.*

Now that the living guards were locked in a cell in the basement, the mansion became their base of operations. The maid, Oksana, showed them exactly where Piper had been held, where they'd eaten dinner, where Ashton slept, where Cain's body had been strung up.

Oksana answered every question with the truth as she knew it, at least according to Brenden's built-in lie detector.

"Ashton bring many women here. He take them upstairs for the night and I never see them again. I no ask questions." She shook her head. "I ask about girl one time," she pointed a finger up, "and I never do again."

"What happened when you asked?" Avery knelt in front of her and put a hand on Oksana's knee. The women still quivered with fear. "It's okay, you can tell me."

Her eyes flickered to Ryse and back. "He make me kill her." Her lips trembled. "He make me take her to monster and push her in the cage. She scream." The woman covered her face. "She scream so loud I hear it still."

"It's okay, let it out," Avery soothed her and held her hands. "Ashton is an evil man, but we'll take care of him. The gods will have their justice."

"The gods do not see him. No one see him. No one stop him."

"I will." Ryse stood tall behind Avery. He had listened, they all had, to her stories. "And you have my word on that. I'll kill that bastard with my own hands the next chance I get."

"You will kill him?"

"Yes."

"Good." She nodded and took a shaky breath. "Good."

It took hours for the guys to gather the intel on all the shipping yards in Nova Scotia alone. Ryse sent Cutter, Philippe, Hammon, and Yankee to all the local harbors to check the ships currently docked, even though they were certain Piper was already at least three days out to sea. If by chance it was a trick and she was somewhere close, they had to double check.

The four Elites went out by car during the night while Ryse, Avery, Nikki, Ixion, Brenden, and Keona stayed at the estate. Brenden and Ixion hunched over computers, Ryse and Keona had an in-depth conversation about every Thracian and person at Evander's estate. Nikki stepped out to the back patio to practice her whip. Avery played with her conjuring ability, creating a plate, a cup, a replica of the keys she found by the front door. Luckily, nothing caught on fire and she didn't have a problem with using up her powers like a candle. Her stomach growled.

"Time for food." Avery popped up off the couch and made everyone else jump. "Sorry."

"You need me to cook?" Oksana asked from her chair. Though Avery had long since put out the fire ring and the dogs were outside with Nikki, she stayed glued to her chair, watching them, answering any questions as they arose.

"Avery can do it." Ryse nodded his chin at her. "I don't need anyone poisoning our food."

Oksana's mouth opened twice before words came out. Her face was gaunt with exhaustion and the crash of adrenaline. "I would never."

"You look tired." Ryse didn't say the words out of compassion, but more of a blunt observation. "Ixion, get one of the dogs to escort her to bed." His attention was right back on Keona.

"I'll help." Avery waved Oksana to come. One of the Dobermans followed them, not aggressively, but attentive of each step made.

"This my room." Oksana pointed to the door, her face turned to the ground.

"Stay here." Avery pulled out a gun, just in case, and opened the room. Unlike the rest of the house, her suite was covered in family pictures, crocheted doilies, a well-used piano in the corner, and collections of miniature bells from across the globe. Her bathroom still had a towel hanging from her last shower.

There were two large windows, but she was on the third story. The only other exit was the door they came in.

"You live here year round?"

"This is my home. Prince Ashton send money, sometimes people, and I take care of house."

"Why? Ashton is a jerk; why do you stay?" She had pretty posh surroundings. Her rooms reflected a woman who had made herself comfortable here.

"I can't tell you."

"I need to know. Consider this a necessity of your survival."

Oksana met Avery's eyes and lifted her chin. "The one they call the Prophet." She took a deep breath. "He is my son. *Was* my son."

Avery's weapon was pointed at Oksana's head faster than she could blink. "Then I think I know where your loyalties are."

"Do it. Kill me." Her body trembled, betraying all the confidence in her voice. "I let my son be mutilated and turned into monster. I know what he is, and yet I serve the bastard who create him. It is punishment for being bad mother."

"Why would you hand your son over to someone using black magic?" Now the dog was snarling, sensing her tension.

"Because he is my prince. What else was I to do?"

"Oksana, I would hate to kill you. But so help me Zeus, if you move one finger against my family, I'll feed your bones to the dogs, got it?"

Her eyes dropped and she nodded.

"That creature killed someone I loved dearly in order to torture me. I will have no problem returnin' the favor." She dropped her gun and stepped back. "Go. And don't leave this room until I tell you to."

Oksana bowed deeply and dodged into her room. Avery pointed to the door and snapped her fingers. "Stay."

The Doberman parked his butt right by the door and lay down.

As she walked downstairs, she considered what to do next. Did she tell Ryse what she learned? Was it really important? Why would Oksana help them unless she wanted them to execute her son?

"Hey." Ryse stood in the hall, watching her.

"Hey." Avery went right into his arms, hugging him close. "You were pretty involved with Keona down there. Everything okay?"

"I was telling her about the Heavens, hoping it made her feel better about letting Evander go." Ryse kissed her head. "I know seeing it for myself helped me to accept my father's death."

Avery raised up on her tiptoes and circled his neck with her arms. "You know what she's goin' through better than anyone."

"I do." He buried his nose in the crook of her shoulder and inhaled deep. "Unfortunately, she doesn't have the promise of his return. It was hard enough knowing you would come back eventually. To lose you for good?" His gigantic body shuddered. "I'd never survive."

His breath on her neck short-circuited her brain. Under her shirt, her breasts tightened and her body ached to be filled with him. "I know where the guest wing is. Oksana said no one ever uses those rooms."

Ryse straightened, his lips pulled back on one side. "You're addicted, woman."

Avery gasped, her mouth open.

"I get it. I'm a beast in the sack, but for the love of the gods, Avery, you may need intervention." The most glorious smile the gods ever crafted spread over his face when she slapped his chest. She pushed away from him.

"Fine, fine. No goods for you, buddy." Avery crossed her arms over her chest and acted indifferent. "I guess I'll just go find a bedroom to sleep alone." She covered a fake yawn and backed away while slowly, teasingly unbuttoning her shirt.

Ryse licked his lips and advanced. "I don't think it's safe for you to be alone. I guess I can sacrifice this once."

The guest wing of the house was never used, according to Oksana, and it showed. Avery noticed a price tag on the pillow as Ryse tossed her onto the bed. They didn't waste time taking off their clothes. If something ripped or a button popped, Avery would just recreate it.

Their mouths melded together in a dance of passion and desire. She loved the way his body felt over her, in her, taking her over with every kiss and thrust. She wrapped her legs around his waist and held on for a long, hard ride. Ryse made her body soar until she felt light as a feather, floating on a cloud. She turned to liquid around him, sighing as he pushed her higher and higher. Sighs turned to pleas to the gods and when she thought she was about to combust, Ryse bent her over on all fours and plummeted into her until they both went up in flames.

Ryse collapsed, panting like he'd run a marathon. "Holy Zeus, it just keeps getting better."

Avery giggled. Her insides were like jelly. "Oh my god. How did you do that thing you did?" She ran her hands through her hair.

"I don't know, I just kind of twisted my hips and…" He blew out a breath, laughing.

"You'll have to do that again."

"Hell yeah." Ryse pulled her onto his chest, both of them still out of breath and sweaty, giggling like teenagers.

"Can you rest with me for a while or do you need to get back downstairs?" Avery gave him her best puppy dog eyes.

"I have my phone if they need me. Let's get what sleep we can before the others return." Ryse pulled a blanket over their naked bodies and Avery closed her eyes, listening to his heartbeat still going strong.

# CHAPTER TWENTY-THREE

## DANTE

ONCE AGAIN, DANTE WAS BENCHED. SURE, THEY WANTED HIM TO stay with Prince Hayden. Sure, they needed someone to keep an eye out on the others. The fact was, his power was once again his downfall. Even Ixion and his dogs were more useful than he was.

General Falcon slapped him on the back and said, "Don't worry about it, soldier. The people left behind need you just as much as the people who left."

Dante nodded and gave him a tight smile. "Of course, sir."

But as he stood in his room, pacing and angry, those words of encouragement didn't mean much. He couldn't even turn to his woman for support due to all the demon blood that now threatened her.

No matter how much it hurt, he loved Lysa too much to put her in harm's way. The thought of anything happening to her made him nauseous. If that beast used him for a direct line, it left him no choice but to keep his distance.

That distance took its toll, even in the short time since he'd walked out on her.

Dante sat on the edge of his bed and put his head in his hands, pressing against his eyes. The image of her naked replayed over and over in his mind. By the gods, she was remarkable. The notion that she wanted *him* still blew his mind. Of all the men in this Haven who would be happy to be her man, she got stuck with him.

His cell phone rang and Hanna was on the other end. "The Lady wishes to see you, please."

"I'm on my way. Dynasty or Lysandra?"

"Both."

Dante considered her words, as everyone should when it pertained to Hanna. She didn't take words lightly.

*Lysa needs me.*

He went to their wing of the palace and down the halls to the Queen's chambers. Hayden sat up in bed, rubbing his neck and talking to his mother beside him.

"She's locked down so tight, I can't get through. It's not good for her to suppress her aura like that." Hayden stood and stretched his legs. "Dante, have we heard anything from Ryse?"

"Yes, my Prince. They found an estate in Nova Scotia and a witness who was most informative. The last phone call I received, they were informed that Piper, Cain, and the Prophet were both on a cargo ship. The Elites are tracking every cargo ship anchored on that side of the country now, then they plan to go to sea."

"I would not want to be that woman," Hanna muttered with a shiver.

"Nor would I." Dynasty shook her head. "But we shall have faith that the gods will keep her safe. Is there any word of the missing Thracians who served Evander? His family is asking."

"Keona only accounted for Nicholas, who was slain in the park, my Queen."

Hayden walked about the room, running his hands through his

hair. "I'm absolutely helpless when it comes to finding her. I've been trying so hard to locate her for days and what good has it done?"

"Don't worry, Prince Hayden," Lysandra offered up her sympathies. "The best of the best are on the case."

Dante's eyes shot to hers for only a second before she turned away. What did that mean?

He took a deep breath and clenched his jaw.

Dynasty caught his eyes and tilted her head to the side. "Lysandra, would you go down to the kitchens and ask Valarie to whip us up something? I'm starving. I know Hayden and Hanna are as well. Dante, why don't you accompany her in case she needs help bringing food back?"

"Of course." He bowed low, knowing that crafty woman knew there was tension between them.

They didn't speak until they were clear of anyone hearing their words.

"What was that supposed to mean?" he said, clenching his fists. "You said the best of the best were on the case, knowing full well I'm unable to go help."

Lysandra turned to face him. "I was including you in that statement. Did you not just deliver news to the Prince? Are you not in contact with the others? I would say you are working the case as best you can."

Dante swallowed, feeling foolish for getting defensive. "Do you hate me?"

"Never." She continued to the kitchen and he scurried to catch up.

"Then why are you acting cold to me?"

This time, she rounded on him so fast, her cape flew out. "Me? Acting cold to *you*?" Flames of passion and anger filled her eyes. "I presented my body to you because I love you and you walked out the door leaving me utterly humiliated and alone with my fears and doubts, which tormented me for the rest of the night and days after."

She advanced on him. "You told me that you loved me. You told me that you would take me as your woman. Then, when the first obstacle came along only moments later, you left me. You walked away, Dante. *You* were cold to *me*." Her eyes filled with wetness, but she blinked it away. "You say you love me, yet you're not willing to fight for our life together. That does nothing to instill confidence in a future together."

Dante's heart shriveled into a raisin. She was so angry she was beyond crying, beyond raising her voice. She was the calm and the storm. "Lysandra, please. The demon—"

"Can't. Hurt. Me." Her words were hard punches straight to his chest. "A demon can't hurt an Oracle. My visions can't hurt me, that's not how they work. And I know you would never let him close enough to try, unless you walk away again. That hurts me more than anything raised from Hades."

Dante realized a cold hard fact about their history. As much as he made her smile, he had made her cry too. "I'm always messing this up, aren't I?"

"We are both learning."

"Yes, but all I'm teaching you is how a man shouldn't act, even if my intentions were for your best."

"Don't you understand, you foolish man?" Lysa placed her hand on his cheek. "My best interest is being with you. I'm safest when you're with me. I'm happiest when I'm in your presence. It breaks my heart when you leave me. The last four days have been more painful than you can imagine." She took a shaking breath and stepped back. "You have to figure out what you want and what you're willing to do about it. I won't shed any more tears for you, no matter how much I want you." She walked off this time, leaving him behind as easily as he left her.

# CHAPTER TWENTY-FOUR

## AVERY

IN THE LIGHT OF THE NEXT MORNING, AVERY WENT SNOOPING; DIGGING through the rooms and bathrooms. For such a big beautiful house, full of big beautiful furnishings, the place was a waste. There was no warmth, there was no coziness, there was no life in it, not like Oksana's room.

There was a sniffling sound coming from one of the bedrooms. Avery stuck her head in and found Keona in a corner, her arms curled around her legs, crying.

"Bless your heart, this must be so hard for you."

Keona's head popped up. She scowled and wiped her nose. "Look, I like you and all, but if you come over here and try to southern charm me out of my only private cry, I might blink you to Antarctica and beat the shit out of you."

Avery chuckled and closed the door. Keona's threats were all exaggerated. Avery saw right through that tough exterior to a woman who had just lost the man she loved and was now afraid her sister would follow. No one faced that without a few tears. Avery flopped down on the floor right beside Keona, who turned her head away.

"Oh, don't act like being southern is repulsive. I bathe and I have all my teeth."

Keona huffed a laugh and leaned her head back against the wall with her eyes closed. "I keep seeing Evander's body in my head. It's like part of me doesn't want to accept that he's gone." Tears flowed down her cheeks. "I loved him so much, and now I'm supposed to do what? Stop? Forget the plans we made? Forget the life we wanted together?" Keona met her stare. "We were going to get married. He wanted kids and dogs and a life with me. How do I turn off those desires now that they've taken root in my heart?"

Avery prayed to Rhea for the right words in this moment; god knows she didn't have them on her own. She took a deep breath and said what the goddess put in her heart. "You don't. Evander's life may be over, but he is with the gods. Even now when you're feeling alone and hurt, he knows. The gods know."

"The gods let this happen. They allowed Evander to die. How can I not be angry with them about that?"

"It's okay to be angry, Keona. It's okay to be upset, it's okay to question your faith and the will of the gods every now and then. They're strong. They can handle it. But you just have to remember that their will is never the death of their people. Never. They don't want to see us sufferin', they mourn when you mourn. The cold hard fact is, we live in a world that provides us with free will, and there are idiots out there who ruin what the gods have created for us. These Rogues, Ashton, Salina, all of 'em—they're selfish. They don't care about other people, only themselves and their own illusions of bein' greater than gods."

"Salina wasn't so great when Ryse whacked her head off."

Avery nodded. "There are always consequences for your actions. No one is above the judgment of the gods, no matter how much they think they are." She gave Keona a pat on the knee. "It's natural to mourn and be angry. It's what you do with that anger that you'll be judged on. Use it wisely."

Keona wiped tears from her cheeks. "We're going to find my sister, right? Preferably before some demon eats her for dinner?"

"My husband is amazing and his men are too."

"Except for Yankee. I can't stand that cocky asshole."

Avery made a snort of agreement. "He's okay. Rough around the edges, but okay."

Keona glanced over at her. "You really do like everyone, don't you?"

Avery smiled, taking it as a compliment, even though Keona's face sneered in disgust. "Not everyone, believe it or not." She took a deep breath and opened up her box of memories to help Keona understand where she came from. "When Ryse found me, I was runnin' my mom's restaurant in Texas. I loved that café, I did. It was my mother's legacy. I lived alone in my childhood home on a cattle ranch, my father's legacy. I had no notion of all this." She raised her hands to encompass the room. "I was fairly happy, I had my best friends, one who worked the café with me, and then there was Frank. He was my big brother, you know? I'm an only child, so I have no clue what havin' a sister is like, much less a twin."

Keona snorted and pursed her lips. "I don't think the world could handle it."

Again, she laughed. No matter how much Keona teased her, there was affection in her voice that made Avery's heart happy. "No doubt. Frank, my other best friend, he might've gone insane if he had to deal with Avery-squared. He was always so protective, so careful with me."

"Was?"

Avery closed her eyes, the memories burned deep. "The night Ryse came for me, our friend, Jerry, got to me first. He was Frank's partner, our pal. He was also a Rogue."

"Damn." Keona sighed.

"Oh yeah, double damn, 'cause I had no friggin' clue what that meant for anyone. Frank came to the house, checkin' on me, and Jerry killed him. He killed him right in front of me because the Prophet was there, coaxin' my powers out of me."

"You had no idea?" Keona's eyes were wide and her mouth open in shock. Clearly, she'd grown up Olympian.

Avery pursed her lips and shook her head. "Imagine my shock when I'm standin' in a room full of men, lookin' like something out of a comic book, and naked as the day I was born."

Keona sputtered. "I'm sorry." She covered her mouth. "It's not funny, and yet, it is."

"It is now, in hindsight. At the time," Avery shook her head, "not so much."

"But you lived through it; that's where this is going, right? You lost your friend, went through some scary shit, and you lived through it."

"Exactly." Avery was quiet for a moment. "I didn't die until later. But, what the corn, I'm still here. So who can really say what the end result will be?" She threw her hands up.

"Has anyone ever told you that you totally suck at pep-talks?" Keona's pretty smile broke through the tears.

"Maybe once or twice." Avery shrugged and they had a moment to enjoy some tear-filled laughter. "What's it like having a twin?"

Keona's face went soft. "It's awesome. Piper is like a mirror image of me and yet so different. It's like seeing yourself in a parallel universe or something."

The thought was enticing, having siblings. Brother and sisters she could run around with and get into trouble with. Maybe the loss of her parents wouldn't have been so hard if she'd had a big brother there to protect her or a sister whose shoulder she could cry on.

"What's it like being a Divine Grace after a lifetime of thinking you were a normal human?"

"It's like being yourself in a parallel universe."

Keona nodded, her lips pulling back in a smirk. She took a deep breath and shook out her hair. "Okay, Keona, get it together. Do I look like I've been crying?"

Avery grimaced. "You appear composed. Except for the red eyes and the snotty nose, you're good."

"Gee, thanks," Keona deadpanned.

"Avery," called Yankee from the hallway. Keona cursed under her breath and turned to face the window.

"In here," Avery called back.

Yankee pulled open the door and examined each of them with his usual irreverence and lack of consideration. "While you guys were in here braiding each other's hair, we think we found a lead at the docks. You coming or you want to stay and paint your nails?" Without waiting for an answer, he turned and headed back downstairs.

Keona glared at his retreating back. "I'm going to strangle him one day, just warning you."

"Ha, get the hell in line, sister." Avery pointed over her shoulder with her thumb and chuckled as they joined the others.

# CHAPTER TWENTY-FIVE



## PIPER

THAT EIGHT BY TWENTY CONTAINER WASN'T LARGE ENOUGH FOR the three people in it, much less the putrid stench of them all after at least three, if not four days at sea. Twice, a man had opened the door of the crate, shoved food in their mouths, and washed it down with water. Hunger and thirst and sickness were her enemies.

The Prophet kept twisting the bars of his cage until the squeaking noise made her jaws hurt and fried her nerves.

Her stomach rolled and churned along with the ship and as much as she wanted to put herself into a trance so she could sleep, the constant unfamiliar noises kept her awake. Contacting Hayden was not going to happen unless she opened up her aura and used her own medical gifts on herself.

Cain desperately needed her help. His breath was so shallow, she had to strain to hear it. She didn't know how much time had passed, but it was completely dark in the crate now.

"Cain?"

"I'm not dead, yet," he whispered.

"I don't think Ashton is aboard. Let me help you."

"No, not with that monster nearby." His chains rattled in the darkness.

"So I'm supposed to let you lie there and die? I don't think so."

"You can't sssave him. You can't sssave yourself." The beast laughed from his side of the crate. "I'll eat you both."

"Shut up," Piper screamed at him, finally losing her cool. "Just shut up, you disgusting creation. Until you actually get out of that cage and eat me, you just keep your damned mouth closed." He hissed at her and tears flowed down her face. "Screw this."

"No, Princess."

"Come over here, stretch out your legs." In the pitch black of the container, she had to stretch out, dangling her body by the arms. Cain was chained slightly further down, so she sought him out with her feet until their legs intertwined. "Is that you?"

"Please don't do this on my account. We don't know where Ashton is. This could be a trick."

"Well, joke's on him. I want you to kill him, do you understand me?"

Piper closed her eyes and concentrated on the steel box in her mind that held her aura. She didn't think twice before mentally opening the lid to the box and letting part of her aura free. After holding it in all this time, it practically took on a life of its own. Cain sighed and groaned as waves of her emotion and power washed over him.

The Prophet screeched like a wounded animal. Piper's aura whirled around the container like the wind before it settled on her and Cain. Now, when she looked at him, she could see his pulse and the miles of veins and nerves and muscles running through his body. She could see the injuries; the broken bones, the burns and cuts, the way his eyes had been sewn shut.

"Oh, Cain." The first thing she did was work on his brain to block the pain receptors. Then she rerouted his blood to avoid the open wounds. He was truly lucky to have any blood left at all. His levels were dangerously low. She sent her aura over his entire body and flooding inside, right down to the cellular level. Piper sent his blood reproduction into overdrive.

"Holy Zeus," Cain groaned. "Thank the gods for your gifts, my kind lady. Thank the gods." His voice already sounded stronger.

"Shh, just relax and let me fix you. I'm going to contact my sister."

"No, she can't come here. If this is a trap…"

"I don't know where we are or where we're going. She couldn't come here anyway. She has to see the place she teleports. I just want her to know I'm okay."

"But," said the creature. Metal hit metal as a piece of the cage came loose and fell to the floor. "You're not okay."

*Keona! Hayden!*

# CHAPTER TWENTY-SIX

## KEONA

KEONA DIDN'T FLINCH AS YANKEE AND BRENDEN INTERROGATED the traitor at the docks. She didn't argue when Ryse's eyes glowed white with the judgment of Ares upon a man who knowingly sent live people out to sea in shipping containers. Neither she nor Avery looked away as Philippe, an Elementalist she did *not* want to mess with, filled the traitor's lungs with water from the bay and drowned him on dry land.

This man knew that Ashton had live cargo and altered ship records to reflect it. He was so proud of the fact he'd done it, he refused to tell them which ship's log he'd tampered with.

"He can be proud all the way to his damn grave," Keona snarled as Ryse picked up the man by the neck and tossed him into the bay. Philippe commanded the waters to take his body far out to the depths where he would never be found.

"Where does that leave us, Bren?" Ryse turned his back on the sinking corpse without another thought.

"I'm going to snoop around and see if I can see the schedule for today. Nikki, I need to blend in, please."

Nikki held out her hands, closed her eyes, and conjured Brenden the same uniform as the traitor; including a name badge. Man, she was a handy chick to have around.

Brenden slipped on the blue coveralls, orange safety vest, hard-hat, and walked off like he knew exactly where he was going. He would use his nose like a dog to follow the trail of the traitor.

"What do we do now?" Keona asked anyone who would answer.

"We wait." Yankee shrugged.

Keona cursed and put her hands on her hips and turned her face to the sky. "There must be something besides that. She's in a crate with a demon. How long can she possibly survive that? Really?"

"Keona, we can't search every ship from here to London. There are laws, risks of exposure—"

Keona screamed and grabbed her head. Yankee caught her as she crumpled to the ground, yelling over and over again. All at once, Piper's aura and emotions hit her with the force of an atom bomb. The initial blast wave of her aura knocked her to the ground. Like a mushroom cloud, the reverberation of Piper's telepathic backlash exploded in her brain. Every emotion, every fear, every ounce of pain her sister had felt for their entire separation blew her off her feet. Keona curled into the fetal position, clawing at her head as if it could relieve the pressure.

Yankee ended up putting his hand over her mouth so she wouldn't be heard and Ryse touched her head, using his aura to pop the pressure valve in her brain. Her body relaxed into Yankee's arms and he stared down at her, terror on his face.

"It's Piper," she cried out, tears streaming down her face. "She doesn't have long."

# CHAPTER TWENTY-SEVEN

## PIPER/CAIN

ONCE THE CREATURE HAD THE FIRST COUPLE SECTIONS OF THE cage twisted out of place, the rest of them didn't take as long. Pieces of the metal bent and gave way and hit the floor.

"I'm coming for you, delicccioussss Graccce."

Piper struggled not to concentrate on him, but on Cain. If she could heal Cain, he could fight the beast and buy her some time to come up with a plan. *Keona is so much better at the plans than I am.*

"My eyes, Princess. I need my eyes." He sounded a hundred times better already. Piper sharpened her focus on Cain to a surgeon's precision. She blocked out everything, including the white noise of her aura hitting Keona with full force and bouncing back to her.

Piper closed her eyes and saw her aura so clearly it was as if she were traveling inside Cain's body. The healing energy traveled up his spine, mending the attached ribs, and into his head, clearing out a concussion like dust with a broom. Her aura and powers reached his eyes. They were sewn shut.

Piper lifted a hand, putting more power out. "This might hurt at first, but trust me."

"I do, Princess."

She infiltrated his skin cells, the ones most affected by the string holding his eyes closed. For only a split second, she caused the cells to separate, ejecting the string and coming back together whole and healed.

Cain sucked in a hard breath and blew it out with each eye she freed. One especially deep stitch had him cussing. As promised, she healed his eyes as fast as she could until he sighed in relief. Once that was done, she headed south.

Another pipe fell from the cage.

"Hurry, little Graccce. The evil demon isss coming."

"You won't touch her, beast." Cain broke the chains binding his wrists to the wall. Piper nearly cried when he held out his hand and his eyes glowed with the white light of the gods. The ankle restraints disappeared for the blink of an eye and when they reappeared, they were just to the left of his foot.

"You're telekinetic!" Piper had forgotten Cain's Olympian gift.

He smiled a perfect, healthy smile as he knelt down in front of her and did the same to her ankle chains. "Yes, my Princess. They sewed my eyes closed because I can't use my gift without them. I only move what I see."

Cain reached up to undo her wrist chains when Piper caught movement out of the corner of her eye.

"Cain!" she screamed.

Cain held up his hands in time to block the beast's claws coming down into his arm. One of the pipes from the cage flew into Cain's grip and the talons were lodged into the metal, not his flesh.

He kicked the demon backwards as it tried to shake off the pipe. Instead, the pipe became a weapon and the Prophet swung it at Cain, over and over, often missing and hitting the sides of the crate. Upon one downswing, Cain caught the pipe and swung around, flinging the pipe and the beast attached to it back against the remaining cell bars.

Cain stood and held out his hands to the chains on the floor. They zipped into his palms like they were magnetized. He squeezed the clamps together into a ball and swung it around like a mace, beating back the beast.

The Prophet screeched and hissed with every blow, backing away, his claw still embedded into the metal.

Once Cain had made him retreat into his cage, he used his powers to send the chains flying towards the enemy. They wrapped around his neck and pinned him to the metal bars.

While the Prophet tried to pry them off, Cain rushed to her side and freed her. "Now would be a good time to contact your sister, Piper." He crouched in front of her, readying himself in case the beast attacked again.

She nodded and sent out a telepathic beacon to Keona. There was a new depth of her strength and once she connected with her twin, she pushed further and tried to reach Hayden, but only Keona answered.

*Where are you? What ship? Are you okay? What about the demon?*

*I don't know where we are or what ship we're on. I just know Ashton mentioned London. I think we're headed there.* Piper cried with relief. Gods, it was good to hear her sister's voice! Hope surged through her and she laughed out loud. *I miss you so much.*

*I'm coming. I need you to keep putting off your aura as strong as you can. Give it everything you've got. Heal the damn whales if you have to, just shine as bright as you can. I'm coming.*

*You got it.* Piper stood on wobbly legs and braced herself against the back side of the crate near the doors. She allowed her aura to retract inside of her again, so that she could heal her own body. Her blood flowed and wounds healed.

As soon as she was whole again, Piper held out her hands, pointed her face to the gods, and let her aura erupt from within.

*My gods, Zeus and your children, fill me now like never before. Give me power and strength promised to a Divine Grace, a child chosen by your hands to do your will. Shine your grace and might through me that none shall be able to deny your authority on this earth. Blessed be your name and blessed be your power.*

Cain stared in awe as Piper began to glow with the light of the gods. Air around her swirled until her hair lifted and her feet left the floor. Her face lit up like a billboard and an angelic smile spread over her face.

She was serenity.

She was the power of the gods personified.

Her eyes opened and looked down upon him. All her body glowed white, except for her black eyes. They were like jewels, shining with darkness.

Cain bowed at her feet, his mouth hanging open like a fool. He couldn't help it. She was beautiful and frightening to behold. "My Lady."

"Stand aside, Cain. I know what I must do." Her voice echoed off the walls. She walked forward, hovering like a spirit. Those black eyes landed on the Prophet, who fought in earnest to get away from her. "You have taken something that does not belong to you and Hades wants it back."

"No, get away. No." The creature bucked and lashed out.

Cain didn't move a muscle. If she was channeling the gods, he dared not interfere.

"You cannot hurt a vessel of the gods. Your greed led you to this place, a place where the will of the gods is defied and mocked. You will be an example for those who think they can defy their maker."

Cain reached out but hesitated when Piper held up a hand and light burst forth, hitting the demon.

He cried out, yelling profanities and struggling to be free of his chains. The red scales that covered his body began to smoke and burn away in places, leaving behind pink skin. The howls and cries of the beast slowly turned into those of a man. The talons shrank away, the snout retracted. His body withered.

Left hanging from the chains was a mutated man with grey eyes and black hair and splotches of red scales. He wasn't completely Olympian again, but he was much less demon.

"What have you done? Look at me! You've ruined me, you've taken away everything." He didn't bother covering himself as he cursed and spit, fighting against his chains. Cain flicked his hand up and a pipe knocked the man over the back of the head and knocked him out.

The light in the shipping container dimmed and Piper was left standing on the floor. She faltered and reached out to brace herself.

"Piper." Cain rushed to her and scooped her up in his arms.

She tried to smile, though her eyelids were lowering. "I hope that was bright enough for Keona."

Emotion hit him hard and knocked the air out of his lungs. If Keona was with Ryse Castille and had access to his tracker, what Piper just did might have saved them both.

He smiled through his tears. "You've done well, Piper. Rest now. I'll take care of you."

He cradled her for a moment as her eyes drifted shut. He laid her down gently, resting her head on his shirt.

Now he had to figure out how to get the hell out of this box.

# CHAPTER TWENTY-EIGHT

## ASHTON

Ashton rolled out of the hotel bed leaving a brunette fast asleep. He answered the phone with a yawn.

"Sir, we have a problem with the cargo."

"What's happened?" His gut clenched. He knew leaving the woman in the container was a bad idea.

"There's light coming out of the container," whispered the man on the other end of the line.

*Oh no.* "It can't be. I sealed it myself. It has wards on it."

"There is light, sir. I'm staring at it now. No sounds, but light. I can feel an aura, it's, wow. It's overpowering me, but none of the other people on the ship recognize it."

Ashton bolted out of bed and rifled through the clothes on the floor. "When was the last time you checked on it?"

"Yesterday, there was no activity. One of the guys on watch noticed it."

"No matter what you have to do, do *not* let anything come out of that container. Text me your coordinates."

Ashton called Xavier and told him to secure a helicopter. He could not lose his cargo. He didn't care if he had to kill every human on board and feed them to his creature.

# CHAPTER TWENTY-NINE

## AVERY/KEONA

NEVER IN HER LIFE WOULD AVERY HAVE THOUGHT IT WAS POSSIBLE for someone to create a speedboat out of pure air.

Yet Nikki could.

The group stood on the dock in amazement as Nikki weaved her hands around in the air and crafted a sea vessel. The blue hull formed along with the motor and inner cabin.

When it was completed, she turned to see wide eyes and hanging jaws.

"Impressive." Ryse was the first aboard.

"I, um…" She swallowed, not liking the attention. "I memorized the schematics of a motor boat as soon as I knew Piper might be on a ship."

Brenden put his arm around her shoulder and kissed her forehead. "Amazing."

Keona was raring to go. She clapped her hands together. "This should be fun. I've never teleported an entire boat with people aboard."

Yankee hesitated with one foot on the dock, one in the boat. "Does that make anyone else nervous?"

Avery thumped his head and pushed him forward. "Behave or she might leave you in the damn water."

"You can swim, can't you?" Keona wiggled her brows and grinned. Now that her sister had made contact, she was a new person. Determination fueled her fire to find the ship.

Yankee didn't appreciate it, but who cared?

Feet pounded on the wood of the pier and Avery turned to see Dante running towards them with a backpack slung over his shoulder.

Avery's heart felt complete with him there. He was one of hers, one of her guardians. She jumped up and hugged him. "What're you doing here?"

He hugged her back and then shook hands with the other guys. "Dynasty and Lysandra both had visions. They sent me out on the first plane."

"What did they say?" Brenden shook his hand. "Will this work?"

Avery should've figured the two of them would be in touch. They were partners of sorts when it came to protecting her. But they would still get a good talking-to when this was over about leaving her out of the loop.

"Keona won't be making contact with me, but the boat. My powers don't act as a conduit through inanimate objects; they can't reach her. No worries." The smile on his face said it all—he was glad to be there, glad to be one of the team again. He held out his hand to Keona. "As long as you're moving the boat and not me, we can make this work."

Keona took a deep breath and shook his hand. "Don't be offended if this is the only handshake you get, then."

"This is going to work. Two very powerful women saw it."

Dante grinned and boarded the boat, making sure he was in a corner all to himself, not near any of the others.

Keona turned to Avery and gave her a smirk, shaking out her hand where Dante had zapped away her powers during their contact. "Now it's a party."

Avery couldn't help but glance around at her A-team. Ryse, who was freakin' awesome, if she did say so herself. Then she had Brenden the shapeshifter, Dante the power canceler, Nikki the conjurer, Hammon the tracker, Cutter the swordsman, Philippe the Elementalist, Yankee the fighter, Ixion and his dogs, and, moving them all at once, Keona the teleporter. Add in her firepower, and they were a force to be reckoned with. Whatever awaited them on that ship, they were more than equipped to handle it.

"Plan, Keona?" Ryse demanded once they were all in the cabin and the motor was running. Not that they needed a captain, but Cutter was at the helm.

"Right. Piper is letting her aura fly free. She's never done that, so I don't know what it might look like." She turned to Hammon, who sat in the corner, already meditating, his eyes glowing with the light of the gods. "He's tracking her. When he gets a direction, I need to be on the bow so I can see what's ahead. We're going to go puddle jumping."

"Puddle jumping?" Cutter asked with a scowl.

"Yes. I'll blink the boat and all of us as far as I can see in the direction Hammon points."

Yankee, who had a grip on the railing, grimaced. "I feel sick already."

Ryse spoke. "When we get close enough to the ship, it is imperative that the humans not be harmed or aware of anything magical happening. We're going to need cover. Philippe?"

The Italian, with his curly hair, nodded. "We move with clouds and fog." He raised his hands to the air and clouds descended around the ship, creating a haze.

"Not too much," Keona warned. "I have to have a clear line of sight."

Philippe nodded once. The fog thinned in a straight line out to the open ocean.

"Once we get to the ship, Hammon has to locate any Olympians on board. Assume all of our people on that ship are not *our* people. If we can hide from the humans, let's do it. I do not want this ship to make the evening news in any country. Everyone understand?"

They all nodded.

"The Prophet?" Avery shivered at the thought of facing him again. At least this time, she was the one on the offensive...and she could burn his lizard-ass into ashes.

"Come, teleporter," Hammon said, his eyes glowing as he rose and exited the cabin, making his way to the front of the vessel and sitting right back down on the deck. He laid his staff in his lap and held his arms up in the air.

"Here we go." Keona touched Avery's arm as she followed. "Everyone make as much contact with the boat as possible. My focus is going to be moving this rig, not individuals."

"For the record, I'm still not confident about this plan." Yankee sat in a captain's chair and gripped the control console for dear life.

Avery tried not to laugh. "What's wrong, Yankee? Don't like boats?"

He narrowed his eyes. "No, I don't like boats and I don't trust her not to leave me in the middle of the bloody ocean."

"Don't you wish you were a nicer person, now?" Avery bit the inside of her cheek to hold in the laughter. Brenden and Dante grinned openly.

"Not a chance." He sneered at them all. "I just wish Ashton would've taken her sister somewhere not covered in fucking water."

Ryse's lips ticked as he met Avery's eyes. He took her hand as they sat together against the side of the cabin wall. Most of the men sat on the floor, making contact with the ship against their backs and legs.

Out on the bow of the boat, Hammon pointed and Keona crouched down, placing her hands flat on the ship. She looked like a runner, waiting for the gun to go off.

"This will work," Dante assured them.

Avery didn't have time to agree. Her universe twisted and contorted into a black tunnel and she clenched her eyes shut.

When she opened her eyes again, they were falling.

"Oh, shit!" Yankee yelled and gripped the console. "Brace for impact."

Keona screamed as her feet came off the boat decking and the entire vessel dropped into the ocean, slapping down against the water so hard she fell and slammed into the wood, landing on her shoulder.

"Ah." She grabbed at her shoulder as pain shot up into her neck and down into her fingers.

"Are you all right?" Hammon helped her to her feet and her arm hung limp at her side. "That's not good."

The teleportation had worked; they were far out into the ocean. Hammon escorted her down into the cabin where everyone recovered from the fall. "Sorry, guys. Next time, I'll aim for the actual water, not the air above it."

"That would be great," Avery groaned as she got to her feet. "I think you broke my ass."

"I think she broke her shoulder." Ryse examined it.

Everything hurt, and her fingers started to tingle from like they were asleep.

"It's dislocated. I need to pop it back into place."

Keona nodded, knowing the burning pain was about to get worse. "Do it. My sister can fix everything else later."

"Take a deep breath."

Keona made eye contact with Avery, who she often looked to for support. She took two deep breaths and stared right into Avery's emerald green eyes.

Ryse didn't take his time. As soon as his hands made contact, he pushed and Keona saw stars.

"Mother fuc-mmmm." She shoved her fist over her mouth, trying to contain all the expletives running through her head, most of which were directed at Ryse.

Once she could see without stars dancing in her vision, Keona nodded over and over again. "Okay, damn, okay. Let's go again."

"Again?" Yankee repeated. "You dropped us out of the sky."

"It was ten feet, maybe." Keona shook out her hands. "I'm the one with a dislocated shoulder. Quit being a wuss."

"Ouch." Brenden chuckled as he helped Nikki sit back down on the floor.

She didn't wait for one of Yankee's smart retorts; she went back out to the bow of the boat.

Philippe joined her. "Which way?"

Hammon's eyes glowed as he pointed straight ahead, slightly to the right. "The signal is strong."

Philippe cast out the clouds in front of them. There was a clear line of sight in front, but all of around them was white fog. If there were fishing boats nearby, they would never see the ship appear or disappear.

Keona placed her hands on the ship's decking, focusing out at the ocean. Her powers connected with the matter in the boat. Running through the wood and metal, the wires and motor, her powers captured the physical properties of her focus.

This time, instead of locking her gaze on the sky ahead, she dropped her eyes to the line where the water stopped and the air began.

*Go.*

The boat went with her as she zipped through space and ended up miles from where she started.

"How far did we go?" Keona asked the guys inside. Cutter, who had gone straight for the controls, used the radar and GPS to figure it out.

"About ten miles from the pier."

"That's it?" Her shoulders fell.

Ixion raised his hand like a kid in class. "You need to be higher. Your line of sight will increase with every foot you are above sea level." He pinched his lips together. "It's simple geometry."

It made sense to Keona. "Okay, everyone get back down. We're going to speed this up. Hang on."

Keona climbed onto the roof of the cabin. It was flat and there was nothing she could brace herself with or hold on to…or was there?

A metal railing grew out of the floor and Keona turned around to see Nikki's head peeking up over the ladder, her fingers waving around.

"Perfect." Keona gave her the thumbs up and Nikki's red hair quickly disappeared below.

Once she had a direction, Keona gripped the bar and focused her energy. Once, twice, again and again, she blinked the boat and its contents across the ocean. Each time took more effort than the time before and only her determination to find her sister kept her going.

Sweat broke out over her face and dripped down her back. Her mind and muscles were exhausted after ten times.

"We're close," Hammon finally said, holding up his hands to make her stop.

"Thank the gods," Keona muttered, all but collapsing against the railing. Her legs were weak and shaking.

Ixion was the first one on the roof to help her down. "That's some talent you have. You okay?"

She gave him a tired smile. "I'm closer to my sister, I'm fine."

He helped her sit down in the cabin. Hammon came back inside with Philippe. "From here, we should let Philippe move us along. We don't need the sound of the motor ruining the element of surprise."

"I'm good with that." Keona leaned her head back against the wall.

Philippe made his way to the roof this time and Keona watched from inside as fog covered them until she couldn't see past the end of the boat.

A wave of energy flooded the atmosphere. Keona sucked in a blast of air. *Piper, I'm here.*

There was no telepathic answer, but the aura rippled with awareness. She'd found her sister.

# CHAPTER THIRTY

## AVERY

AVERY NEARLY PEED HERSELF WHEN OUT OF THE FOG APPEARED A ship that made their boat look like a bath toy. The gargantuan cargo ship left a wake that should've sent them away in a hurry. Philippe had them far enough away that the clouds still provided cover.

"Hammon?" Ryse motioned to the ship with his chin. "See anything?"

"There is a burst of Olympian magic from the starboard bow. I see one other aboard. He's at the stern making his way forward." Hammon pointed to the places on the ship, and good thing he did, because Avery didn't speak sailor.

"Threat level?"

"Low. He's a water power, but not a very strong one. Nothing compared to Philippe."

"Here's what we do: Hammon, Avery, Keona, and I will board the ship, find the girl, and radio back."

"I should go." Dante stepped forward "At least according to your mother."

"I can't teleport you up there." Keona wasn't focused on him. Her eyes were glued to the ship.

"No, but you can teleport Hammon's staff and I can hold it."

He'd figured out his loophole and now there was no reason for him not to be there.

"Same principle as the boat; let's do it. I think I see an opening."

Avery and Ryse touched Keona's arm, Hammon handed her his staff, then touched her elbow. Dante gripped the staff.

Being in direct contact with her was much easier than the boat had been. Within the space of two heartbeats, she stood on the deck of the cargo ship. Ryse ushered all of them behind one row of the containers and they crouched down.

There were no voices coming from the ship, just eerie silence. "D'you think they know we're here?"

Ryse shook his head. "Look."

Avery's eyes couldn't pierce the fog to see the motorboat, though she knew it was there.

They moved quietly down the row of containers and crouched down before crossing an open area. Hammon signaled the clear for them to cross and keep moving. With each row of containers they passed, the powerful aura grew and strengthened.

Along with the clean, crisp, bright aura that she assumed was Piper, there was an evil one.

The familiarity of it made her nauseous. It took her right back to that night at her house when the red-scaled monster ruined her life.

The bright aura faded and Keona gasped. "Something's wrong. We have to hurry." She picked up the pace and Avery stayed right behind her.

"Wait," Ryse pinned them both to the side of the container. "Listen."

Avery's heart thudded in her chest as the whirling rotors of a helicopter approached.

"Hurry." Hammon led the way to the final stack of shipping containers.

*Boom. Boom. Boom.*

The sidewall of the bottom crate bulged out with each thundering bang. With the fourth boom, a bloodied fist burst through the galvanized steel.

"Thracian," Ryse said as he took the lead. He spoke into the hole. "This is Ryse Castille. Name yourself."

"Master," the man cried out with relief. "I'm Cain, a servant of your cousin, Evander. I have a Divine Grace here, Master, and the one they called the Prophet."

"Back up, soldier." Ryse held out his hand and the sword of Ares materialized, one of the gifts from the gods. He raised the sword and brought it down, slicing through the steel like butter.

Ryse handed off his sword, then used his bare hands to pull back the sides of the container.

"I hope he's gentler in bed," Keona said with wide eyes, her aura rippling with a hint of awe. She jumped into the container without a care of what might await her. "Piper! Cain!" Keona ran to her sister and picked her up. "I'm taking them to the boat."

"Go." Ryse didn't hesitate.

The three of them blinked out as the helicopter whizzed overhead and turned to face the container, blowing water and air all around.

"Ashton," snarled Ryse. He stood in the opening, the ocean spread out before him, and Ashton's helicopter hovering right in front.

The guns on the helicopter aimed in their direction.

Avery stood beside her mate, her hands already flaming with fire. He wasn't about to get to Keona or Piper again.

"Father?" Dante's jaw tensed as he saw Xavier sitting in the pilot seat. "That bastard."

Behind them, chains rattled and Avery turned to see the Prophet, or at least, that was what she thought it was.

"I've got him." Dante grabbed him by the neck.

"Dante, no." Her heart nearly burst apart in her chest.

"He must die. It's why I'm here." Dante wrestled the man into a chokehold. His gift of canceling powers made the man weak as a baby. He brought the demon spawn to the edge of the container for Ashton to see. "Set him on fire."

"You're holding him. I can't do that," Avery said out of the side of her mouth.

"Yes, you can. Trust me and if not me, trust Lysandra."

Avery held up a flaming hand and pointed it at the screaming lizard man. He cussed and kicked, fought and screamed, but he was no match for Dante.

Ashton held up a hand and Ryse groaned in pain. "Do it fast."

As much as she wanted to help her mate, Ares would protect him. Ashton might think he was a match for Ryse, but he wasn't, not by a long shot.

Ryse used his sword as a shield, deflecting the bullets with lightning speed. Ryse tried his hardest to cover them all, but bullets sprayed the side of the ship and the container in all directions.

If she was going to kill this demon, she had to do it now.

"This is for Frank." Avery pressed her hand over his mouth and sent her fire right down his throat. He burst into flames from the inside out, pushing Dante backwards, right into the opening of the container. Dante went down, two blooms of red coming from his chest. He fell into the back wall, out in the open.

"No!" Avery lunged for him as a bullet hit her left arm and she fell back for cover. "Dang it."

Ryse's body crumpled, his arms shaking as he tried to combat Ashton's attack.

Avery dodged another spray of bullets, then leaned out the door hole and sent flames streaming towards the engines of the helicopter. She pelted the rotors with fireballs until it spun out of control.

"We have to jump," Ryse screamed, grabbing Dante with one hand and her with the other. They took a running leap out of the container and off the side of the ship. The last thing she heard before she hit the water was the helicopter smashing into the containers.

# CHAPTER THIRTY-ONE

## PIPER

THE BOAT BOUNCING OFF THE OCEAN WAVES WOKE PIPER UP. SHE blinked her eyes into focus to see the crying face of her twin sister.

"Keona," she whispered and tears filled her eyes. "Cain?"

"I'm here, my Princess, thanks to you." His bright eyes stared down at her, his body was healthy and whole.

Piper covered her face and cried, so overjoyed she couldn't express it any other way.

There was commotion as the boat slowed down.

"He's been shot. So has she."

Piper sat up, even when Keona urged her not to. People were in pain; she had to react.

Off the back of the boat, men pulled in three people, two of which were unconscious. Piper crawled to them, the man first. He was bleeding from his chest. Piper scanned his body and saw the two bullets. She poured her aura into him and ejected the bullets and fixed the tissue. Her powers pumped into his heart until it could beat on its own.

He coughed and gasped, raising up and grasping at his chest. The other men ushered him into the cabin of the boat.

The woman had swallowed water. Her lungs were almost full. Piper pressed on her chest and commanded her lungs to expel the water and inhale air. She also had a bullet wound to her arm, an easy fix.

Once the woman gasped for oxygen, Piper gave her some room.

"Avery? Baby?" A big man, no, a *huge* man, picked up the petite woman and cradled her head in his arms.

*Avery?*

*Ryse.*

Piper scurried away to the safety of her sister's arms. Keona held her close. "It's okay, he's on our side. Or, we're on his, rather."

Avery fumbled into the cabin and downward, out of sight.

Ryse Castille met her eyes and she covered her gasp with her hand. *He has the same eyes.*

His huge shoulders lifted and fell with a heavy breath. A familiar smile crossed his lips. She knew that smile from her dreams. "Welcome aboard, Piper. Hayden will be most excited to see you. Keona, let's go home."

Keona wiped the tears from her face and nodded. "Yes, sir."

Piper sat on the floor of the boat beside Cain, surrounded by people she didn't know, people who had risked their lives to come rescue her.

"Here we go. Everyone, hold on."

"Oh gods, not again," said a brutish looking man hugging the control panel in front of him. The other people on the floor chuckled.

Piper was all too familiar with the teleportation process and was not surprised when her reality twisted and became something different.

The boat splashed down and gently rocked over to the side, sending them all falling to the right.

"Oops." Keona giggled as she stuck her head back in the cabin, crawling over the door. "Guess I should've asked how deep this pond was. I'll take care of this later, I promise."

Cain carried Piper off the beached boat, through the pond, and onto dry land.

The scene surrounding the pond was pure beauty. Rolling hills, lush gardens, and in the middle of it all stood a castle that made her jaw drop. "We're in a Haven?"

"Yes, my Princess," Cain said, holding her against his chest.

"I've never been to a Haven." Hope spread a smile across her face. Cain placed her on her feet, careful to hold her arm when she swayed.

They walked up a cobblestone driveway to the palace as maids and butlers came rushing out. In the middle of the chaos, Piper's breath caught.

Stepping out the door of the grand castle was a man who she never thought she would truly see with her waking eyes.

He was tall and thin, not bulky like his brother. His black hair hung to his shoulders, just like she remembered. And when his chocolate brown eyes met hers, they widened and a smile so blindingly beautiful spread across his face.

Before the thought settled in her brain, her bare feet were moving, taking her to Hayden. He ran down the steps of the palace and across the driveway.

"Hayden, Hayden!" She cried his name as she dodged a maid and leapt right into his awaiting arms.

"Piper, holy Zeus, you're here. You're real. Dearest gods, you're real." He buried his face in her hair and sobbed right along with her.

Her knees gave way and he went right down to the ground with her, both of them crying and touching each other. She had to feel his clothes, his hair. Piper's cautious heart had to make sure she wasn't dreaming again.

"I'm here. I'm here with you." She laughed, happiness overflowing her heart.

"You're with me, really with me." Hayden held her face and kissed her cheeks, her eyes, her nose, then rested his forehead on hers. "You're here."

Piper didn't know if she needed to laugh or cry, so she did both.

"I love you," she whispered. "I loved you before I knew you."

"I love you too, angel. Now that I have you in my arms, I'll never let you go as long as I live." Hayden pressed his lips to hers and kissed her like never before. This wasn't a kiss of desperation or separation. It wasn't from a man whose existence she once doubted. It wasn't from a ghost who visited her dreams in the dark of night.

This kiss was from a living, breathing man who the gods created just for her, whose black hair shined in the sunlight, whose pulse beat wildly under her hand, and whose lips promised forever.

She didn't know what else the gods had planned for her, but at least she knew she would face it with Hayden and Keona by her side.

She turned her head to see her twin linked arms with the auburn-haired woman from the boat. They both had tears in their eyes and happy grins on their faces. Beside them stood the mammoth giant who looked like Hayden. He took the woman by the hand and nodded to his brother.

"Everything is going to be okay now." Piper met Hayden's beautiful eyes and hope blossomed in her chest. The gods had fulfilled their promises. She was home.

Coming next

JOANNA GRACE
DIVINE
DECEPTION
THE DIVINE CHRONICLES BOOK 6

# ABOUT THE AUTHOR

JoAnna Grace lives in a world of alpha males and strong females where true love conquers all—at least in her books! From the time she started holding a crayon she began to create magical worlds. Living in the real world was never an option. A proud indie, she has published over a dozen novels including The Divine Chronicles series, The Blake Pride series, Riverview Romances, and more. This writer loves to read contemporary, paranormal, and urban fantasy romance novels.

JoAnna's tales are spun at her home in East Texas where she lives with her Prince Charming, three kids, and a few dogs and cats. When not hiding behind the computer screen chugging coffee, you can find her having fun with family and friends, singing, camping, or managing multiple businesses.

Connect on social media!

Like, Follow, Tag Jo, and share this book with your friends.

Instagram @authorjoannagrace
Facebook @joannagraceauthor
Goodreads: goodreads.com/author/show/7173373.JoAnna_Grace
Bookbub: www.bookbub.com/profile/joanna-grace

Make sure you're in the know. Sign up for the newsletter today!
http://eepurl.com/B_DM5

Do you want to help an author? Leave a review
Your opinion matters.
Every review can help.

# Pride Before the Fall

## BLAKE PRIDE SERIES

# JoAnna Grace

# PROLOGUE

V IVIAN BLAKE KNEW THE MOMENT SHE'D BECOME MORE than just another dominant female tigress. It was the moment her muzzle became covered in the life blood of her alpha, a male lion twice her size. His sadistic games had led to her captivity and near insanity. Now she'd overpowered him and others were watching, waiting for her command. Those four lives might not have been many compared to the hundreds of Pride members, family and friends they had left behind, but Vivian would kill a hundred more alphas if it meant protecting them. This was her new family, her new Pride, and God help the bastard who dared to take them from her.

# ONE

KASEY BLACKBURN SAT BEHIND HIS EXECUTIVE DESK AND peered at the five people in front of him. To the untrained eye—or nose—they might have appeared nervous. But he knew better.

These five people were not nervous.

They were alert.

Their eyes noted the four other men in the room standing guard. Every exit had been memorized. Every object that could be used as a weapon had been cataloged. Predators.

However, Kasey was just as observant. Sitting in the middle of the three women was a tall, statuesque dame with seductively powerful brown eyes—their alpha. She sat proud and straight with her legs crossed. Vivian Blake. Bountiful in every way, the woman had curves that made his blood boil. From her reddish-brown hair in a long ponytail to the miles of jean-covered legs, she was built strong and hard. If he were completely honest with himself, she was the sexiest damn woman he'd ever seen. It took monumental self-control to keep his arousal in check. There were nine other shifter noses in the room, after all.

"What can I do for you, Miss Blake?"

"We came to let you know we will be residing near your territory for an unknown length of time."

Kasey leaned back in his chair, casually resting his chin on one hand. "Where exactly?" He fiddled with his tie like he couldn't care less about them. The truth was quite the contrary.

"We've rented a space above the Chinese restaurant on 8th."

"You haven't done your research, Miss Blake. Blackburn territory covers the entire city. It also extends into the mountain and includes most of the state forestry land."

Luscious lips pinched together and her jaw tightened. "That's quite a spread. We were told the bears controlled the mountains."

"They do. And I control the bears. They joined my Pack a few years ago."

"Well, good," said the feisty blonde sitting on Vivian's right. "I do hate making two of these calls." Amilynn, who was number two or three in the small Pride, was a loaded gun waiting to go off.

The busty sex kitten looked ready to fuck or fight anyone in the room. He'd noticed all his men had given her a second glance when she sauntered in and flipped her abundance of blonde and black hair. It didn't help that she was wearing a naughty school girl costume complete with the short plaid skirt and matching tie hung loosely around the opened top buttons of her white shirt. The black nail polish and combat boots were a contradiction but suited her more than the skirt. She couldn't have been a couple inches over five feet tall but, then, dynamite came in small packages, too.

Kasey sat up and put his elbows on his desk. "Vivian, I'm afraid I can't offer your Pride sanctuary here."

"We don't need your protection," barked out the blonde. She received a quick glance from Vivian and it was enough to quiet her.

The feline alpha spoke as calmly and respectfully as she could, given the circumstances, "All I am asking is that you allow us to stay here for a while and work."

Alias, one of Kasey's council members, spoke up. "The Blackburn Pack does not harbor fugitives."

Vivian speared him with a hard, steady glare. "You haven't done your research either. We aren't fugitives."

"Maybe other alphas you've visited aren't as well informed as I am. I know who you are and why you left your Pride." Kasey pinned Vivian to her chair with a look, yet she didn't waver in her eye contact.

With her chin lifted slightly, she replied, "We simply left our Pride on bad terms and they've held a grudge."

Kasey laughed out loud. "Bad terms?" He laughed again. "That's putting it mildly, don't you think?"

"With all due respect, Mr. Blackburn, you weren't there. You cannot begin to understand the reasons why we left, so don't try. Now, can we stay in your territory for a while or not?"

"How do we know you're not a threat to us?" Sampson, Kasey's Beta and brother-in-law, spoke just as rationally as Vivian. There was no bitter taste to his words. It was a genuine and legitimate question. Vivian had killed her alpha after all.

"We don't want trouble. We just want to work for a while."

Kasey studied the group for a moment. Behind the explosive Amilynn and the barely controlled Vivian stood a male the size of a Mack truck—all muscle, not an ounce of fat on him. Conall. He stood with his hands stuffed in his pockets. He remained quiet but his square chin pointed high and eyes that had seen too much scanned the room every few seconds. Military trained, if Kasey had to guess. He didn't have to do anything but stand there to be intimidating. He was the muscle where Amilynn was the mouth.

On the female alpha's left was the only submissive in the group. The petite young woman was related to Vivian, sisters based on facial structure and similar scent, though they looked little alike. Melissa cast a softer impression with bright blue eyes and long black tresses that faded into a deep burgundy. She was a modern Snow White. Where Vivian was tanned, Melissa had a milky complexion with glowing pink cheeks. Her right hand rested on Vivian's arm. The touch of a submissive was calming to more aggressive personalities.

Behind Melissa stood a man Kasey had kept his eye on from the moment he'd walked into the room. Tyrone was a walking shadow. He prowled silently as he had entered and had an aura of darkness about him that was frightening even to a man like Kasey. His head was covered with a solid black hat that barely showed his eyes. All of his black clothing was baggy enough to hide weapons underneath. What little skin was showing had tattoos. He looked more thug than soldier. The only thing that Kasey saw as a weakness was the way one of his hands rested on Melissa's neck, his thumb stroking over her pulse. They were a mated pair, but how? One was a ray of light and one was the very shadow she cast.

"Vivian, I find it hard to believe that we won't have problems. Even though my men searched each of you upon arrival, I know at least two of you remain armed." He shot a look at Tyrone and Amilynn. His man at the door came over and Kasey raised his hand to stop him. The guard stood beside Amilynn. "Am I wrong?"

Amilynn looked up at the man and gave him a smile that could have seduced even the Pope. "I guess you'll have to search a bit more . . . *thoroughly* next time, big boy." She giggled at the guard as he swallowed a lump in his throat. Martin was an excellent soldier, but this woman challenged his stoicism.

When Amilynn turned her gaze to Kasey, it held none of that sensuality and all of the danger of a predator. "You'd be a fool to think we would go anywhere unarmed." She tilted her head in a feline manner. "Not that we need the weapons to protect our alpha." She leaned back in her chair and crossed her black combat boots.

"I'm sure you don't." Kasey laughed off her performance. He didn't give two shits about her silly threat. She was the decoy anyway. It was the one in the middle who interested him. The exotic looking female had taken on her previous alpha and left him one heartbeat away from death. This was the woman he needed to pay attention to. No female should be able to take on her alpha and win. He looked at Vivian giving him a lazy, confident grin. "What kind of work?"

"We were scouted by a club manager here. We're musicians, performers."

"What club?"

"Does it matter?" Vivian tilted her head to the side.

"Yes, actually. I own several businesses around town, including a nightclub or two."

"Bristow's. He saw us while on vacation in Vegas. He offered us more money. We came."

"Bristow's, huh? Not one of mine. Surprising that he offered you money at all. You must be impressive."

"We have our skills."

Amilynn looked over at Martin and said, "On and *off* stage."

Kasey couldn't help but grin at the way Tyrone rolled his eyes discretely. He took a deep breath and held it for a second before letting it out while he analyzed the dynamic of this Pride. Vivian and Amilynn: dominant, unmated females. They clearly made the decisions for the group. Melissa was fragile. Fear in her eyes indicated she'd been hurt and it made sense now that she gravitated toward the strength of Tyrone, an assassin as deadly as a man could become. Conall was the odd man out. He smelled of both the unmated females, so he either lived with them or was sleeping with them both. No, not that. Two dominant females would never share a male. He was the protector of the protectors.

"Six months probation," Kasey said, rising from his chair and buttoning his dress jacket. Vivian rose with him and her Pride with her. "When was the last time you ran?"

"I only ask for a once a month free run."

Kasey looked up at her with brows dipped low. "Is that all you've been getting? Once a *month*? No wonder you are all barely contained! Is this what you call leading a healthy Pride, Vivian?"

Vivian hissed at him and for a brief second her cat shone in her eyes. She stretched out her fingers that had already shifted into claws. "I do the best I can with what I'm given. The last territories we were in bordered cities: Minneapolis, Vegas. Hunting was harder. We were only granted free runs once a month. We got used to it."

"You can't stay human that long. It agitates the animal and, as you just displayed, makes them surface harder and faster. It makes you dangerous. You have once a week runs in the forest. Sampson."

Sampson pulled up a map and showed them places where they could freely shift and run. It was a vast area. The look on Vivian's face said she was relieved. He took this moment, when she was bent over a map on his desk, to get an eyeful. Under the black leather dress jacket she wore nothing but a white tank top that hugged the curves of her modest breasts and showed off the flat plain of her stomach. Jeans accentuated wide hips and lush thighs. Her hair spilled over her shoulder and his fingers longed to muss it up.

Control. Damn it. He had to keep control. One wrong scent or look and things could go south quickly. "Take your family out this weekend," he said as everyone straightened.

"Thank you." Vivian stuck out her hand cordially. "You've been generous and we won't forget it."

Kasey took her hand in both of his, stepped up close and looked into the bedroom eyes of a dangerous cat. And damn if that sexy feline didn't hold his stare like the powerful alpha she was. Deep within him, his wolf awoke. Here was a woman who challenged him, defied him in front of his men, and yet the bastard wanted to mount her right there. The wolf wanted to give her something. He wanted to show this woman he could provide for her. "If you need anything, call me."

"I can handle my own, but thanks." She turned to leave and he couldn't help but be thankful for the chance to see her walk away.

As the Pride filed out, Sampson noticed that Melissa had left a sweater hanging over the arm of her chair. He picked up the sweater and approached the woman with a shoulder tap. In less than a blink, Tyrone had a knife to Sampson's throat and Melissa safely tucked behind him. Kasey stepped in just as Vivian touched Tyrone's shoulder.

Sampson held up his hands in surrender, showing the sweater. "I just wanted to give her this."

"No one touches her, *ever.* Got it?" The man's voice was rough like the sound had to pass through a layer of gravel in his throat.

His mate's voice was a soft, sweet soprano. "Ty," Melissa whispered, slowly walking in front of him and taking the sweater. "Come on, baby, it's okay. He didn't know." She gave Sampson a nod of thanks, then touched Tyrone's cheek. The adoring smile she gave him could move the earth. "He just surprised me. It's okay. Let's go." The cat's hand moved so fast Kasey didn't see where Tyrone stashed the knife. Without another word, Melissa led him out of the office.

"I'm sorry. I should've warned you. He's rather protective," Vivian said after they exited the room.

Sampson brushed it off. "As any man should be with his mate."

With another nod to Kasey, Vivian Blake left his office. It would be weeks before her scent would leave his thoughts.

www.ingramcontent.com/pod-product-compliance
Lightning Source LLC
Chambersburg PA
CBHW050358190726
48284CB00007BB/2346